PRAISE FOR *GONE BEFORE YOU KNEW ME*

"*Gone Before You Knew Me* is more than a great YA novel. It is a great any-age novel. Wildermuth's characters crackle off the page, flawed humanity in all its glory. The tone is fast and smart, a present-day cousin to Raymond Chandler or Megan Abbott, with whom she shares a great eye for detail. Like her story's protagonist Talya, Wildermuth is what Shakespeare would have called a first-class 'snapper up of unconsidered trifles,' and an author with the skill to weave those tiny, telling moments into a riveting story of school corridors and spy rings."

—Brendan Foley, creator of the CW's *Sherlock & Daughter*

"Renate Wildermuth has the recipe for a truly great book. She starts with dynamic characters, adds intriguing mysteries, whisks in radical plot twists and a full cup of killer action sequences, then tops off her marvelous concoction with delightful doses of clever humor, perceptive insights, and the perfect pinch of romance. *Gone Before You Knew Me* is an absolutely winning read from first sentence to last, an irresistible world I'd eagerly return to."

—Neil Connelly, author of *Into the Hurricane*

"Not your everyday outsider girl surviving high school story—not by a football field. Twists and intrigue speed down the hallways, along with teen angst and humor. Talya's voice doesn't just sing throughout but resonates with life, questions, and all that comes with growing up."

—Patricia Marcantonio, author of *Best Amigas*

"*Gone Before You Knew Me* is a gripping tale of survival and grit. Talya's acerbic wit and painful memories make her a riveting narrator to this powerful adventure. Are her deductions the imaginings of a troubled teenager or an observant young woman? Fans of Alex Rider and *The Hunger Games* will find her a compelling character. Wildermuth's reveals spring at readers to astonishing effect as she weaves the strands into a satisfying plot."

—Nev March, award-winning author of *Murder in Old Bombay*

"A mysterious opening, an exciting ending and a whole lot of smart writing in between, *Gone Before You Knew Me* is a terrific read. I won't soon forget Talya, the book's gutsy high-school heroine, and her intense story. Renate Wildermuth has written a winner."

—Ken Jaworowski, Edgar-nominated author of *Small Town Sins*

Gone Before You Knew Me

Renate Wildermuth

Fitzroy Books

Published by Fitzroy Books
An imprint of
Regal House Publishing, LLC
Raleigh, NC 27605

https://fitzroybooks.com
Printed in the United States of America

ISBN -13 (paperback): 9781646036844
ISBN -13 (epub): 9781646036851
Library of Congress Control Number: 2025937267

Cover images and design by © studiochi.art

Printed in the United States of America

Regal House Publishing, LLC
https://regalhousepublishing.com

To Mrs. Reafler, my first favorite teacher,
and to teachers everywhere.

THE END

(AND THE BEGINNING)

I don't know where I am, and no one else does either except for the guard escorting me into the interrogation cell. I focus on the badge on his uniform that says *security*.

"Ironic, isn't it? That a secret agency uses labels," I say. He doesn't crack a smile, but my dislocated shoulder makes a popping sound as he shoves me down onto a metal chair. He throws a notebook and a blunt pencil onto the steel table in front of me.

"They want your story of how the homecoming game became an international incident."

I still don't know who *they* are.

"My hand's broken," I remind him.

"Use your left."

"It will take forever."

He shrugs as if to say that's the amount of time I've been allotted.

My story? I don't know where to start. What unfolded today was set in motion before the game ever started. I stare at the blank page so long I begin to imagine one of Mr. Ebert's motivational posters: SET YOUR SIGHTS HIGH; AIM HIGHER.

The guard sets the sights of his pistol in the middle of my forehead. I realize I'm holding the pencil like a knife. He has more imagination than I gave him credit for. The pen may be mightier than the sword, but I don't think a pencil will ever trump a Glock.

Mr. Ebert told our twelfth-grade English class the most important sentence in a story is the last one. How does it end? Is Axel still alive? Do I have his blood on my hands? Literally, yes.

The pencil's sticky as I reposition it awkwardly in my left hand. Figuratively?

How does it end?

"You tell me," the guard says.

"Is he dead?"

He shrugs again. "Which one are you referring to?"

I decide I'd rather not know.

I turn to the two-way mirror on the cell wall. My reflection gives me a withering look then glances away, like she doesn't want to get involved. She's had enough. I don't blame her. I observe her from the corner of my good eye. She looks like ██████. Half her face is covered with a bruise. The other half with blood. She's hunched over.

"The shoulder," I guess. She nods.

The guard pulls my wrist straight out and twists. The ball of my arm bone drops back into its socket. I don't say thank you. Neither does my reflection. She sucks in a ragged breath and turns a mottled gray. She looks like she's about to cry.

Axel never loved you, I tell her, to turn the sad into mad. I don't know if it's true, but it works. The color comes back to her face. She throws me a look of pure venom.

I hate you, she says.

"It's mutual," the guard replies.

"I wasn't talking to you."

"Right," he says. Or *write*. It's impossible to know for sure.

He presses the cold barrel of his gun against my temple for clarification. I know from my training a Glock is a locked-breech, semi-automatic weapon. It also happens to be a highly effective writing prompt. I know in a flash exactly how my story begins. With a cliché: the day Axel walked into my high school English class and changed my life forever.

And his life? I don't know if it's over. The suspense is a killer.

Maybe I am too.

Subject Name: Talya X.

Location: ████████

Record Group No. 1

I had about 6,936 hours to go until I graduated from high school; if you don't want to do the math, it was the first day of my senior year. It was a miserable day in the town of ████████. The weather was lousy too. Outside the window, the sky looked like it had been beaten black and blue and would give up the rain any minute. Lightning was electrocuting the thin edge of the horizon.

But in Mr. Ebert's English class? There was not one spark of curiosity. It was the last class before lunch. I heard the occasional stomach grumble. Or it could have been thunder. Ebert was trying to explain to us what a cliché was. It was like pulling teeth.

Then the new student walked in fifty-three minutes and twenty seconds late. He did to the class what the lightning was doing to the sky: he made it come alive. I'd remember later that lightning could also incinerate things.

Mr. Ebert introduced him as Axel Hemmings and went on with his lesson. Now everyone was paying attention, as if it was something you actually had to pay for. We all watched as Axel slid gracefully into the only open seat in the back, between Tommy and Kamal. Kamal had been featured on the front page of the local newspaper for being the first and only exchange student we ever had. The article said he came from a small kingdom on the other side of the world. It didn't mention why he'd been banished to a place like ████████.

And Tommy? We don't call students gifted anymore; Tommy was exceptional. He exhibited signs of severe assholism. I didn't need to be a medical professional to know it was incurable.

Mr. Ebert had moved on to metaphors. He told us a metaphor compares two unlike things that deep down have something in common. Tommy and Axel had absolutely nothing in common. Tommy's slouch came naturally. Axel had to work at it. Tommy's stringy blond hair hid his glassy eyes. Axel's jet-black fringe barely brushed his deep brown eyes shaded by thick lashes. I wrote that all down as fast as I could.

I kept detailed notes on everyone and everything that went on in ████████. It wasn't as difficult as it sounds since nothing ever happened there. I kept my observations in a college-ruled, spiral-bound, five-subject notebook with a red cover. I considered it to be a kind of dossier, not that I would have ever said that out loud. I rarely said anything out loud.

I opened my dossier to a blank page. I studied Axel. I'd known him for forty-three seconds and already I felt I could write a book about him. I pretended I was reading the poster above his head that said: THERE'S WORK IN TEAMWORK FOR A REASON. He struck me as the type of guy who preferred to work alone. He had at least three years on us. I could tell by the five o'clock shadow on his chin. Most guys in the class hadn't gotten past noon.

He wore a black ACDC shirt, brand-new, like off the shelf. I transcribed in detail how it strained against his biceps. He stretched out a graceful leg, long enough to kick a hole through my peripheral vision. I wrote: *High-tops: brand new, no scuff marks. Well-fitting jeans. Holes torn on purpose?*

I noted Chatham's reaction. He was the captain of the football team. A crease had appeared in his smooth forehead. He wasn't looking at Axel at all. He was staring at his girlfriend Darcy who was a cheerleader. She was the one ~~looking~~ gaping at Axel.

You're wondering why I kept a dossier? Mrs. Hawkins, the

school counselor, would tell you because of past trauma I was emotionally detached, that I used the dossier like a shield. It put distance between me and my classmates. She told me I was an observer of life because I was afraid to live it. In truth, I kept the dossier because I didn't belong here in █████. I'd been taken out of my old life suddenly and violently and put into this one. I was looking for the crack in the façade, some clue as to how I got here and more importantly how I could get out.

Nothing was as it seemed. No one was what they seemed. Except I was pretty sure about Mrs. Hawkins. She was into healing stones and useless phrases. She told me it was okay to be human. I was more human than she'd ever know, but I knew better than to show it. She said I should let my light shine. In high school?! That's like putting a candle in your window during wartime in a blackout. It's a sure way to get obliterated.

Nobody noticed me. That's how I liked it. That's how I was going to make it out of high school without scars, or at least no more than I came in with. I was five foot six, had brown hair in a ponytail, brown eyes, brown-rimmed glasses. I dressed like I forgot to change at the end of gym class: gray sweats, black athletic tank top, and a gray zip-up hoodie. I was a standout in fading into the background.

I finished my detailed description of Axel. Nothing about him added up, from his made-up-sounding name to his unscuffed shoes. *NARC?!?* I wrote tentatively. Before my pencil left the page, I knew that wasn't right. I felt a tingle on the back of my neck, a premonition, an awareness.

I turned to look at Axel again. He was staring at my dossier. Then he looked up directly into my eyes. I stopped thinking at all. I want to say I was a deer frozen in headlights, but Mr. Ebert would have called it a cliché. We were supposed to be writing as many metaphors as we could in five minutes. Axel's gaze was intent, like a laser that zeros in on a target a split second before the target gets blown away. When his eyes narrowed, I stopped breathing. Then he smiled. It was a lazy, spontaneous, smoldering thing. The corner of his lip curled up like paper touched by a lit match. That doesn't mean I started breathing again. Which probably caused the physiological response that the rest of the class noticed.

"Talya's blushing!" Tommy said. "Can computers blush?" He continued in a stilted robotic voice. "The epidermis of my facial area is reaching critical temperature. These feelings do not compute. My processor is being fried. Does not compute."

I knew about bullying, but I kept such a low profile I never thought it could happen to me. It was unsettling. Painful. I didn't deserve it. The things Tommy deserved I wasn't capable of dishing out. But the universe has a way of doling out justice.

I'm not saying it was karma that slammed Tommy's head into his desk. I just never actually saw Axel's hand move. I heard a thud and Tommy's nose started gushing blood like a fountain. That was a cliché, but it wasn't wrong. His Pink Floyd shirt was turning a darker shade of pink. Axel hauled him up by the back of that shirt, saying something about "helping" him to the nurse's office.

On his way out, Axel reached for my dossier with his free hand. I pulled it to me, and his smile widened. That spark that had touched the edge of his lips was spreading like a wildfire. He winked at me. This time I felt it, the widening of my capillaries in response to adrenaline.

I blushed again. So what? I'm human.

The one good thing about high school is that almost all of us have had that traumatic experience. So, I can say my school was exactly like yours, just take away a few fluorescent lights and add a couple glass cases full of trophies. Cut the school library hours down to one day a week because of budget issues. Put the school in a rural community with six warehouses, four churches, three bars, two banks, and one convenience store. Give it a brand-new state-of-the-art football stadium. [redacted] like any other small town had its priorities. You can probably guess where I spent most of my time, or would have, if it had been open more than one day a week.

I wasn't born in █████. I ended up there after my parents were killed in a carjacking when I was fourteen. I was in the back seat. You can imagine a lot of things change after something like that. Mrs. Hawkins said I might be able to get into college by writing an essay about it, since I didn't have much else to recommend me besides good grades. She said I was lucky. I wish her all the luck in the world.

I was at lunch after English class when she called me down to her office. I never ate in the cafeteria. It scared the █████ out of me which is saying something considering I survived a carjacking. I would let myself into a supply closet to make notes in my dossier while I ate my sandwich of white cheese on white bread surrounded by discarded blackboards. I had found a stick of chalk when I'd first arrived, and I marked the passage of days in █████. I'd chalked up 1,059 tally marks so far.

No one ever noticed I was missing from the cafeteria or anywhere else. When I heard my name come over the loudspeaker summoning me to the guidance office, I dropped my last nub of chalk. It shattered on the dusty floor of the closet.

You can imagine Mrs. Hawkins just like your school counselor with wispier hair. She was busy being mindful when I walked into her office, so I sat in a cushioned chair hugging my dossier to me while I listened to her breathing deeply. The healing stones she wore around her neck grated on each other with every exhalation. I wondered why she'd want to be weighed down like that.

She had a miniature fountain on her desk with recycled water running endlessly over smooth rocks. Layers of folders had built up around it like sediment. It appeared to be eroding down into the surface of the desk like the Colorado River into the Grand Canyon.

I didn't realize she was done being mindful and had opened her eyes, or that the metaphor had made me smirk.

"The sound of running water makes me happy too. So, Talya," she said, beaming at me. The healing stones jangled around her neck like they just couldn't contain themselves for joy. "Axel was asking about you."

"About me?"

"He asked for help with his disability."

"His what?"

"I can't tell you what it is. Privacy concerns. I've given him access to the conference room next door so he can withdraw whenever he needs to."

"What does this have to do with me?"

"You're intelligent in a way."

"In a way?"

"In an intelligent way. Axel has social intelligence. You both stand to gain so much from each other."

"Does he want me to tutor him or something?"

"Oh, Talya, I hope it will come to that." She clasped her hands to her healing stones. They shuddered in expectation. "For now, he'd like to see your notes to get caught up."

"It's only the first day," I reminded her.

"It's never too early to not fall behind." She removed the dossier from my grip with a strength and speed that surprised me. I would have made a note of it, but I had nowhere to write it down.

"I think things are going to turn around for you, Talya."

I had that feeling too, that they would go from bad to worse.

I had inherited nothing from my parents except my mother's cheekbones and what my father had taught me about how to survive in this world. Stay alert. No detail is too small to notice. The dossier was my link to him. It was the closest thing to a family heirloom I possessed. I had to get it back.

Axel didn't show up for civics after lunch. Tommy returned

with gauze stuffed up his nose and a crooked smile. I could tell he had self-medicated and was feeling no pain. His eyes were two glazed donuts against the pale plate of his face. As he walked by me a cloud followed him. It smelled like pixie dust and unicorn dreams.

I would have opened my dossier to write that down. Then I would have flipped to Axel's page and crossed out NARC. If he wasn't here to bust a drug ring and take Tommy away, why was he here?

After civics I had study hall, but I didn't go. It was like lunch except without the chance of a food-fight breaking out. A small consolation. I returned to the solitary confinement of the supply closet.

At the end of the day, I spied Axel coming out of the conference room. I'd been waiting for him, but the school was emptying like someone had pulled the plug on a drain. Not being noticed worked for me most of the time, but nice words spoken in a soft voice didn't exactly part a crowd.

I caught up to Axel in the parking lot. He was standing next to a nondescript black sedan that looked brand new. It was conspicuous for its inconspicuousness. He looked me up and down. My heart began to race. He wasn't admiring my curves. I didn't have any. He was assessing me. A strange feeling began to hum across my nerve endings. Not just because he saw me; I saw something in him that I recognized.

"What do you want, Talya?" He remembered my name!

"You're looking for something. For someone. That's why you wanted my dossier."

He smirked. "That's what you call it?"

"It can't be something that's already happened. Nothing ever happens in ████████. They think something *will* happen, don't they?"

"They?"

"Your people. Whoever sent you here. You're some kind of agent."

"And you're a girl with an overactive imagination."

"I'm an observer. And I'm not a girl. I'll be eighteen in 121 days and six hours."

His smirk grew wider.

"Tell me why you're here, what you're looking for in my dossier. I can help you!"

"I'm here for an education. I want to know where the cool kids sit at lunch. Get acclimated."

"You don't belong here," I said.

"That's rude."

"I didn't mean it like that. I don't belong here either. I'm not supposed to be here. I just woke up here one day."

"Like you were dropped here by aliens?"

"Not aliens. At least I don't think so. I never saw them."

"Don't tell me you're allergic to kryptonite. I bet you have superpowers."

"I'm invisible," I said.

Axel tilted his head. "You know I can see you, right?"

"What I mean is I'm the kind of student teachers mark absent when I'm there and present when I'm not. The only people who really see me are Mr. Reynolds, because I made the mistake of asking questions in world government last year, and Mrs. Hawkins. But she sees what she thinks I should be."

"Hmm mmm," he said noncommittedly.

"We can help each other. I can go places, do things that you can't because no one notices me. You stick out. You're too tall, you're too good-looking. You attract too much attention."

"Thanks for the compliments."

"Just objective observations," I said.

He nodded, but his strong brow furrowed, and his well-formed lips were pursed in a way that said they doubted that.

"Here, you can have your dossier back."

I snatched it away from him. I'm not afraid to admit I hugged it briefly before opening it and paging through it, looking for something I may have missed.

"Is it a plot to overthrow the government?"

He didn't answer. I knew he wasn't a NARC, but [illegible] was located at the intersection of two major interstate highways. What had brought Tommy here last year for the brisk drug trade, could attract other actors as well.

"Gun smuggling?" I guessed. "Or witness protection! Is someone hiding out here? This would be the perfect place. No one would ever look. Not in a trillion years."

"You're going to miss your bus. It looks like rain."

I never took the bus. It was a mosh pit on wheels with the only adult literally looking the other way. I glanced up. The air was thick and moist, the sky gritty, like a dirty sponge about to be wrung out. Lightning struck beyond the football stadium. As Axel opened the car door, a lightbulb went off in my head, because the dome light didn't go on. "You've disabled the overhead light."

He shrugged. "Maybe the bulb blew."

"It's a brand-new car. You did it on purpose, so the light won't give you away at night. You're a spy. I'd bet my life on it."

"Because I wear *un-scuffed sneakers*?" He quoted my dossier, adding a laugh. He was watching the cars leaving the parking lot, his eyes moving methodically from driver to model of the car before scanning the license plates.

"I smell it on you," I blurted.

"Like what? I'm wearing 007 cologne?"

"It's the way you carry yourself, like you're expecting someone to come at you. It's the way your eyes never come to rest. You're looking for anything that's out of place. You're not just looking around, you're assessing threats."

His eyes narrowed as he turned to assess me.

"You've been watching too many movies."

"I know it from experience."

"You know a spy personally?"

"My father was a spy." I had never said it out loud and it came out almost as a whisper.

"Really? Who did he work for?"

"He didn't talk about his work."

"But he told you? He said straight up he was a spy."

"Not exactly," I said as I looked down at Axel's un-scuffed shoes.

"Let me guess, he would disappear for long weekends and come home smelling like secret agent perfume? I'm sorry to have to tell you this but he was a normal guy having an affair."

My head came up. "He loved my mother!"

"I didn't say he didn't."

"There were other clues. We lived off the grid."

"Maybe he was a hippie, or a prepper."

"He taught me how to pick locks."

"Did you ever think locksmith? Or thief …" he offered.

"We moved constantly."

"Sounds like he was easily bored."

"He had passports for different countries with different names, but it was always his face on the photo."

Axel cursed softly. "Your father was a conman."

I stared at him. It was all I could do.

His voice lost its hard edges. "Maybe his biggest con of all was convincing his daughter he was some kind of secret agent."

It started to rain. A drop of water hit my cheek and fell like a tear.

"I'm sorry to break it to you, but maybe now you can move on," he said.

Move on? My past was crumbling around me. I was trapped in the rubble.

"Go, Talya, please, before you get caught out in the storm." He looked up at the darkening sky, got into his car, and I watched him drive away. I know now a storm was coming. It had nothing to do with the weather.

I didn't cry. If you don't believe me, you can check the forecast that day. It was the sky that wept in heavy drenching sobs. The rain was so thick I couldn't see the car crawling along beside me down the suburban lane until the honk of the horn startled me.

The tinted window slid down.

"Get in, before you drown," Axel said from the driver's side of his nondescript sedan. "I'll take you home."

"I don't have a home. It's my uncle's house," I said as I settled myself in the passenger's seat, the new car smell being eclipsed by rainwater and mud. I had shoved my dossier under my tank top to keep it dry. It was stiff as armor as I clipped the seatbelt across it.

He sighed. "Okay, then, I'll take you to your uncle's house."

"He's not my uncle."

"So, he's a friend of the family you call 'uncle.'"

"You should start with him."

"What do you mean?"

"As a suspect."

"Here we go again," he muttered.

"He gets paid to watch me."

"Sounds like a full-time job."

"I don't think he really exists. He's a plant."

It sounded like Axel had begun to pray.

"He wipes down everything he touches. I'm telling you he is working for someone. KGB, OSS."

"Sounds like OCD." Axel shrugged.

"I'm not making this up. I think he was assigned to me after my parents were assassinated."

He blew out a slow breath. "Mrs. Hawkins told me your parents were killed in a carjacking."

"That's how they wanted it to look."

"Hmm hmm."

He pulled up in front of my house. I saw the curtains flutter.

"Did you see that?"

He shook his head. He was staring out the windshield.

As I got out, the rain felt like tiny fists beating on my head. "We can help each other. I can get information for you. You can help me get out of here."

"I think you do need help, Talya, but it's not the kind of help I can give you."

"I don't belong here!"

"You think you're the only one? Everyone's trying to fit in in high school."

That wasn't what I meant. He didn't stick around to hear an explanation. His taillights threw a red shadow onto the wet pavement as the sky sputtered.

I let myself into the house of the man who was not my uncle. He was standing by the bay window in the living room. His outfit never changed, carefully pressed dress slacks and a white button-up dress shirt that could barely contain his bulging neck and thick shoulders. His hair was black as shoe polish and as shiny. He had a mustache to match. It was thick and protruded like someone had left a broom in the middle of his face.

He didn't greet me as I stood there dripping on the mat that did not say *welcome*.

"Who was that?" he asked me.

"The new kid."

Before he could ask me more about Axel, I had questions of my own.

"I want to know where my parents are buried."

"Why?"

"So I can visit them."

"What's the point?"

"Closure."

"They were cremated."

"I want the ashes."

"They were scattered."

"Where?"

"Into the wind. The past is the past." He looked down at the water pooling around me. "Don't make a mess of things, Talya. Not now."

I had my dossier back and nothing else. My parents had been scattered to the wind. Mrs. Hawkins wanted to fix me. The only person I had ever confided in, Axel, thought I was crazy. My uncle was not my real uncle, not even my family of choice. I think deep down he wanted to kill me sometimes.

Something was coming, something was going to happen in ████████. Whatever it was, it was big, a rising wave. Maybe I could ride that wave out of the life I lead there. If Axel wouldn't tell me, I'd work it out on my own.

I spent most of that night going over every entry in my dossier. I won't write out all the details here, not with a broken hand. I'm not saying my classmates weren't important, it's just that most of them are not central to this interrogation.

Every school has the same kinds of students in about the same ratio of bullies to nerds. ████████ wasn't any different. We had the kids who were open books of tattoos no one could read. The emos who didn't give a damn what anyone thought of them and wanted desperately for us to know that. Then there was the guy who let his T-shirts do the talking. They were usually saying insensitive things.

It was a thing in ████████ to name your kids after towns or give them last names for first names. This seemed to afflict members of the football team in greater numbers than the general population. Like Chatham. And Henderson, Atkins and Carson. They're going to be important later on.

There was one girl in ████████ who didn't belong to any of the groups but navigated them all. She seemed kind, open, and interested in the world. She had noticed me when I came to ████████. She had smiled at me twice.

The first time, I was so surprised my mouth dropped open in surprise. The second time it happened, I was prepared. It took effort, but I willed the corners of my lips to go up. That time her mouth opened in surprise and her eyes widened with what I can only describe as fear. She never looked directly at me again.

I tried the expression out later on my reflection. She bared her teeth in a horrible grimace. I couldn't tell if she was mocking me or wanted to bite me.

Who needed friends? I had my dossier. I could tell it anything. It didn't judge me. I knew it inside and out. I noticed that Axel had earmarked some of the pages. The corners were no longer bent, but I could see the indent where they had been. I still didn't know why Axel was in [illegible], but I now knew whom he was there for. There were three people he was interested in.

I was not one of them.

RECORD GROUP NO. 2

Axel skipped chemistry the next day. I knew he'd be there for Ebert's English class again because he'd earmarked Ebert's page in my dossier.

You can imagine Mr. Ebert's classroom exactly like this concrete cell I'm in now, only with windows and motivational posters. GOALS ARE DREAMS IN WORK CLOTHES for example and DREAM BIG. WORK BIGGER. Ebert was going to have to work a lot bigger to get out of ██████████ to get a job he was better suited for. He had a loose gray ponytail, wire-rimmed glasses, and a peace sign tatted on his wrist. He had ideals. But the ideal teacher for that class was a police officer not a peacenik.

I glanced back at Axel. He didn't notice me, but Tommy did.

"You look like you had a rough night." I pretended he wasn't talking to me until he threw some paper at me. In book form. It was a paperback—*The Jungle*. It's about the horrible conditions in the meat packing industry in Chicago, but that title could easily describe any high school. It hit my upper arm and landed on the floor with a thwack.

He leaned forward. "Were you up late getting your software defragged?"

"Shut up, Tommy," Axel said.

My heart sputtered like an engine that hadn't been started in a long time and was trying to turn over.

Mr. Ebert was teaching us the difference between free verse and blank verse. The class was looking back at him with blank stares. Our assignment was to write a poem that didn't rhyme. One came to mind immediately. *Roses are red. I hate school and Tommy.*

Mr. Ebert wrote *onomatopoeia* on the board and asked for a definition. I knew it was a word that sounds like what it describes, but sheesh, I wasn't going to call attention to myself by raising my hand.

"I can give you an explanation," Tommy said. Every head swiveled in his direction. He paused for dramatic effect, then he farted so loud it could have registered on a Richter scale. Mr. Ebert shook like he'd felt the tremor. I watched his face fall the way a building collapses in a quake. The façade was gone. I saw a flicker of despair and something like hatred before he turned back to the board and rested his head against it.

I glanced at Axel. His eyes were on Ebert's hands. They were clenched into fists. How far would Ebert have to be pushed to snap? Had he already snapped?

Most of the class found the whole scene incredibly humorous judging by their guffaws. Was that onomatopoeia? There was no way I was going to ask. I couldn't bear to see Ebert like that, so I looked at the poster above his head. LIFE IS LIKE A PENCIL. IT'S UP TO YOU TO LEAVE YOUR MARK WITH IT. When he straightened up, I noticed his forehead had left a smudge on the blackboard. I wondered if he ever imagined that's how, as a teacher, he would leave a mark. He murmured something about silent reading, went to his desk, opened a book, and pretended to read. The class didn't even pretend.

After a while he put the book down, pulled a legal pad from his desk and began to write manically, his pencil never leaving the paper, as if he were writing one long word.

Finally, the bell rang sending us all back to our corners for the next round.

I saw Axel get a look at the legal pad on his way out before Mr. Ebert shut it up in his desk drawer. I hung back and took a look myself. It was difficult to read, except for the last sentence that was written all in caps and underlined. *WHEN THE SMOKE CLEARS THOSE KIDS ARE GOING TO THINK DIFFERENT ABOUT ME*.

I followed Axel into the conference room. He was looking at

his phone and he put it away as he sensed my presence. I was able to get a glance at the display. It looked like multiple screens of live footage, like from surveillance cameras. I looked at his sneakers. They were scuffed now and muddy. I imagined how he had spent his night after the rain had stopped, going around town and the school hooking up spy cameras.

He sighed as he took a corner seat at the conference room table. I noticed he was positioned so that he had a clear view of the door and the bank of windows. Across the small room was a wide framed mirror. Below it read: *You're looking at the love of your life and your best friend.*

I glanced at my reflection. She stared back with a strained smile as if to say we were acquaintances at best. She looked away as I took a seat next to Axel.

"What are you doing here, Talya?"

"It's not Ebert."

"I have no idea what you're talking about."

"I know he's one of your suspects. I'm telling you it's not him. I saw what he was writing."

"How could you? He locked it up."

"I told you I know how to pick locks. He had hall duty after class. I went through his desk."

He didn't believe me, so I opened my dossier and wrote in what I'd seen. His eyebrows went up in surprise.

When the smoke clears those kids are going to think different about me. I read it aloud and tapped a pencil against it. Shouldn't there have been a comma after the word *clears*? "There's something that's bothering me about it."

"Yeah, that it sounds like a threat."

"But it doesn't sound like Ebert."

"How?"

"I can't put my finger on it yet, but I know it."

"Oh, I get it, he doesn't smell like a suspect. You know what, I did some research yesterday. There are no records on you."

"Doesn't that raise a flag?"

"Yeah, one that says you don't get out much."

After what happened to me, I had chopped off all of my hair and most of my name. My hair was more than long enough now to put into a ponytail. Some things don't grow back.

"I used to be Natalya. Now I go by just Talya. I use my mother's maiden name. If you did another search—"

"There was no carjacking. Certainly, no assassination."

"I can prove it!"

"Talya, there's nothing you can say to convince me."

I didn't say a word. I pulled up the hem of my tank top to expose my stomach below my breast, just above the swell of my hip.

If I didn't convince him, I know I surprised him. His eyes widened. He bent his head toward the scar on my side. It was about the size of a dime but not as smooth around the edges. His attention was as searing as the interrogation lamp in this cell. I closed my eyes. As so often happened, the memories came back to me in a sudden, violent flashback.

When I became a teenager, my parents decided I should have normalcy. We reentered society, moving into a condo just outside our nation's ██████████. I went from living in deserts and jungles to reading about them in out-of-date textbooks in a suburban high school. I was supposed to take the bus, but with the amount of traffic, the five miles took me less time on foot. Riding the school bus was like living the sequel to *The Lord of the Flies* and the sequel is always worse than the original.

I had about 34,392 hours to go until I graduated (roughly translated, I was a freshman), when my parents picked me up from school out of the blue. I got my hopes up we were leaving, but I didn't see any camping supplies or provisions.

My father had a meeting near the planetarium. He and my mother thought it would be a treat to take me to the afternoon show. The streetlights in our neighborhood drowned out everything in the night sky. My parents knew how much I missed camping out under the stars. Seeing a projection of stars plastered onto a concrete dome was sooo much better than seeing the real thing. Yes, that was sarcasm. I'd been in high school twenty-seven days. I was bound to catch it.

I asked my parents when we'd be going back to our old way of life. They said we'd be staying where we were for good. *Good* is not a word I would have used.

My parents asked me how school was. I told them it was normal. I didn't tell them normal sucked.

I wish now that hadn't been the last thing I said to them. Why couldn't I have said, *I love you* or *I'll never get over losing you.* That would always stay true. But *normal*? Nothing would ever be normal again.

I had a good idea what profession my father was involved in. I'm sure he could have extracted more out of me than one word, and without leaving marks. He just sighed, while he and my mother exchanged a pained, knowing look.

They talked to each other about my father's new job. He never used the real names of the people in his line of work. He called them things like McGillicuddy. At first, I had found it funny, but 216 hours of high school had dampened my sense of humor.

It was always hot in that city and muggy. I sank down in the backseat until I could only see sky from the car windows. The radio called the traffic stop and go. This was all stop. We rolled the windows down. Because our lives seemed so *normal* now, my parents must have also let their guard down. I don't blame them. Not completely.

Two figures all in black with face masks to match came from nowhere. That's a cliché, but I can't explain it any other way. Suddenly, they were there on either side of the car, holding short-barreled rifles. They fired simultaneously. They used silencers. I can tell you from experience that doesn't completely silence noise, in fact experts call them suppressors. Technically they muffle sound, like the muffler on your car does.

When I think of that day, a line from a T.S. Eliot poem comes to mind: *This is the way the world ends, not with a bang but a whimper.* There was no super-sonic boom, my parents just turned into rag dolls. I was the one to whimper.

The masks swiveled toward me. The one on the right—who had just shot my mother—cursed.

"There wasn't supposed to be a kid," he said. He cursed again. The word felt like an assault. Still, it was nothing compared to the impact as his partner—without a word—turned on me and fired.

When I woke up, the doctors told me I had been lucky. The projectile had gone clean through without hitting any vital organs.

I never wanted to be "lucky" again. I wanted to be prepared.

I had never told the story to anyone. I hadn't used that many words at once in a long time. "Do you believe me now?" I asked Axel in a hoarse whisper.

His silence spoke doubt. I couldn't bear to look at him. I kept my eyes screwed shut. So, it came as a shock when he reached out to touch me, rubbing a thumb over the scar as if he could erase it.

My eyes flew open. I sucked in a breath like my heart had just been restarted with a defibrillator. That bullet hadn't killed me, but I realize now I'd been dead inside until that moment. Emotions that had atrophied began to tingle, sensations and feelings pulsing through me, burning along my nerve endings. My reflection shuddered. I did too because I saw something in her face that frightened me. She was coming alive. She was going to stay alive, no matter what the cost.

I'm not saying what happened after that was Axel's fault. Not exactly. Was Dr. Frankenstein to blame for what he brought to life? It was technically his monster that wrecked a village and hurt a lot of people. In the end we'd have that in common.

Without removing his hand from my stomach, Axel looked

into my wide eyes. I saw doubt in his, and maybe some pity, but also curiosity. He opened his mouth to say something at the very moment Chatham walked into the conference room.

"Am I interrupting something?" Chatham asked.

"No," I said.

"Yes," Axel said.

I yanked my tank top down, trapping Axel's hand under it, giving a completely different and more intimate impression than me just showing him my scar. Which admittedly was pretty intimate to begin with. I'd laid myself and my past bare. I felt like if I looked down, I'd see a new scar left by the imprint of Axel's thumb.

"What do you want?" I said to Chatham. "I mean, why are you here?"

"Mrs. Hawkins said you're tutoring."

"Don't you get straight As?"

He shrugged his linebacker shoulders. Maybe things didn't come as easy for him as I thought. He sat down on the other side of the conference table, so the three of us made a triangle.

"I just don't understand this whole free verse thing for English. It would be helpful to have some parameters."

"That's the whole point of it, to not have parameters."

"What does that even mean?"

I looked into his bright blue eyes. It was like gazing into a sky completely empty of clouds. I looked to my dossier out of habit and paged through as if I could find a way to explain it to him.

Chatham. He'd been born and raised in ██████. His father had played football, like his father before that. He was bred for it, shoulders like a wide timber, but he tapered at the waist and had long legs for speed and agility. He'd been the quarterback since he was a freshman. He got up every morning before sunrise, lifted weights and ran before school started. His diet was carefully calibrated with a strict ratio of carbs to protein. He never strayed from it.

Axel's page came next. There were so many blanks to be filled in. He was a mystery I couldn't quite solve. He was a question not an answer. I realized I was pressing a hand to my scar as if his thumb had opened up a wound, and I was trying to keep myself from bleeding out.

"How do you know?" Chatham asked.

"How do you know what?"

"If someone writes something in free verse, how do you know it's a poem, not a paragraph?"

"Like you know if you've been hit by lightning. You feel a shock, before it sizzles along every nerve and sets your cells on fire like a torch falling onto dry brush. It obliterates everything you ever knew, turning your world into an empty husk, so some new awareness can come out of it, a new way of seeing and being. It's excruciating, yet it's beautiful too, and…" It struck me I might be overexplaining.

The room was completely quiet. I looked up. Chatham was staring at Axel. Axel was watching me, his eyes wide as if he was impressed by the depth of my passion for literature.

"Do you get what I mean?" I asked Chatham.

"I think I'm starting to understand."

Axel's lip quirked like he doubted it. They held a brief staring contest. They didn't like each other. I could tell things like that from the tenseness in their shoulders.

Axel leaned forward. "I heard something's going to happen at homecoming."

Chatham shrugged. "We're playing our biggest rival. There are always fireworks."

"I heard Kamal is planning something." Axel hadn't heard it! He had read it in my dossier.

"You'll have to ask him." Chatham got up and went to the door.

"I'm sorry," I said. "I didn't do a very good job of explaining things."

He turned back with his big, graceful hand on the door handle. "No, it's fine," he said to me, but he was looking at Axel. "I found out all I needed to know."

I felt bad after he left. Is that how Mr. Ebert felt after class all the time? Teaching someone a lesson was not easy. Not at all. But I felt worse about what I had inadvertently done to Kamal.

I flipped to Kamal's page in my dossier after Chatham was gone.

"Kamal is not planning something bad at homecoming," I told Axel.

"I never said he was."

"You're watching him. I saw the CCTV footage on your phone."

"I like reality TV," he said, neither confirming nor denying he was spying on Kamal. I knew he was, and it was my fault.

I scanned through Kamal's entry in my dossier.

Six foot two inches, brown hair, golden-brown eyes. Born in the Kingdom of ████████. Four trips to the ████████ since arrival in junior year. He lived with Chatham and his family. The two had become as close as twins. They could have been brothers. They had the same powerful yet graceful build and they both lived for football. They differed only in skin tone and hair color—oh, and Chatham drove a pickup, not the Mercedes. And Kamal wouldn't eat pork. That bothered some people. It seemed Axel was one of those people. I scrolled through the page with my finger, stopping at the latest entry from yesterday. In chemistry class, which Axel had missed, I overheard Kamal say something to Chatham. *I'll show them. After homecoming they won't be able to ignore me any longer.*

I looked up at Axel. "You're reading it out of context."

"What was the context?"

"I don't know, I didn't hear the rest of the conversation," I admitted. "I just know he's not going to do whatever you think he's going to do."

"Is he a friend of yours?"

He had never said a word to me. That was true of 99 percent

of the student body. That didn't make him a bad person. That made him normal.

"No."

"Let me guess. He smells innocent."

"You're seeing something in him because of where he's from. That's profiling. It's illegal."

"You can't see what's right in front of you."

"I notice everything." I put my hand demonstratively over my dossier.

"But you don't really see."

"It's the same thing."

"Is it? What about Chatham?"

"What about him?"

"Exactly my point."

"You're confusing me," I said.

Axel reached forward and took my glasses off, sliding them carefully down the ridge of my nose. It's not the sexiest place to be touched, that piece of cartilage, but if you're not used to being touched at all, it can feel almost erotic.

He held my glasses up to the light before focusing on me again. "Just like I thought. These aren't prescription. You don't use them to see, you use them to keep from being seen. Chatham sees you." His eyes narrowed. "He sees those full lips. Those doe eyes. Those cheekbones. They're so high, you could bungee off them."

Axel was no Shakespeare. Shakespeare was dead, British, and from the few sketches of him I'd seen, not very good-looking. He confused me too. That was the only thing they had in common.

He set my glasses back on the tip of my nose and pushed them gently back up. I was holding my breath, maybe that's why I got dizzy.

"But you don't notice Chatham noticing you."

"Chatham? He's the most popular guy in school."

"I never said he wasn't. You don't see and you can't hear what I'm saying."

Part of me, a very small part, say 10 percent, thought that could explain why Chatham had just come in for tutoring when he was a straight-A student. The majority of me, the other 99 percent dismissed it. I realize the math doesn't add up. I'm not a robot, but the human brain runs on electrical impulses. My mind, like any other circuit that gets overloaded, had been blown by what Axel was saying.

I don't want you to think I had a self-image problem. I had a non-image. From my first day in high school, I'd seen how cruel kids could be to someone who stands out. I strove to become the human embodiment of camouflage.

Mrs. Hawkins took that to mean a lack of self-confidence. She was big on loving yourself. About that? You can't have both parents die before your eyes and not have some tiny irrational part of you hate yourself. I know I didn't pull the trigger. Just like other kids "know" they're not the reason for their parents' divorce.

If I couldn't love myself 110 percent, I at least liked myself. As a friend. The fact that I had no friends is a topic for a therapy session, not an interrogation.

I was lost deep inside myself for a few moments, like how when the lights go out, you rummage around in the basement looking for the circuit breaker. Like flipping that switch, a mental light went on.

I blew out a breath I didn't even know I'd been holding. "Ohhh," I said slowly as my thoughts started powering up again. "I get it. You're trying to distract me."

Axel sighed. He leaned forward for emphasis. "Read my lips. Chatham sees you." His eyes moved over my face, then dropped to my mouth. He blinked. "And I—" he began.

"What?" I whispered. He didn't finish his sentence. His half-smile had flatlined.

Are the children of spies marked in some way, a barcode imprinted into our irises? I thought maybe, just maybe he believed me. He shook his head as if to clear it, and my heart sank.

He pulled back, putting distance between us before the bell even rang.

"See you around, Talya."

"You're trying to confuse me!" I said as I followed him to the door. "Is that something they teach you? I'm not going to fall for it. You've got your sights on the wrong person. I'll find the real suspect on my own. When I do, your people will have to help me."

He sighed and raised his eyes to the ceiling. He pulled his phone from his pocket. "You know what? You're right. You got me. I'm exactly who you say I am. I'd show you my spy badge, but my organization is so secret they don't even have a name. I'm going to take a picture of you. I'll feed it into my Spyscanner 3000. It will match you against our database of espionage offspring." He held the phone up to my face. I didn't hear a click. Maybe he had disabled the tone. Maybe he didn't actually snap a picture. Maybe he did.

"I'll let you know as soon as I find something out. Until then it's best you pretend you don't know me. If this whole operation goes south, it's safer for you that way, okay?" He gave me a conspiratorial wink and let himself out of the conference room without waiting for an answer.

I was embarrassed by the state of my reflection. "You know he's trying to get rid of you," I chided her. She nodded, but I could see in her eyes part of her hoped he really had taken a picture and there really was a Spyscanner 3000. I felt sorry for her, but I couldn't afford pity.

"Get over it. No one's going to solve your problems for you," I said harshly. "Your glasses are askew," I added. She reached up with a shaky hand to right them. I couldn't bear to see what she did next. I had to look away.

Record Group No. 3

My uncle kept to himself. So did I. You'd think we would have been a good match. You'd be wrong. Neither of us had ever had a visitor in the 25,440 hours I'd lived in his house. I'd never even heard the doorbell before. When it sounded at ten p.m. that night, I jumped like I'd been shot and raced down the stairs.

My uncle got to the door before I did. Axel stood under the porch light, his arms crossed over a Metallica shirt. I felt a sudden surge of excitement and hope. It felt surprisingly similar to a stomach virus.

"Hey," he said. "Can Talya go for a walk with me?"

"You can ask her yourself, I'm not her warden," my uncle said. His tight smile was like a razor blade showing under the rug of his carefully clipped mustache.

Axel put out his hand. "I'm Axel. I didn't catch your name."

"I didn't give it. It's John Smith, but you can say uncle." I'd read enough books to recognize the phrase, saying uncle meant *I surrender.* I could tell from Axel's expression he didn't understand until my uncle took his hand and squeezed. I saw Axel's bicep ripple, saw his jaw tense with strain as they battled it out in a barely concealed arm wrestle.

I pushed my way past my uncle, forcing him to let go. "I'll be back soon."

"You're free to do what you want," he lied, as he watched us go.

We walked to the end of the block under the dim streetlights. Axel's car was parked along the curb. He opened the passenger side door. "Get in," he said tersely.

He sat in the driver's side flexing his right hand as if it were sore, staring down the block at my uncle's house.

"You don't exist," he said.

I had felt that way for the past 1,060 days, but it didn't feel good to hear it said out loud.

"I know. I wasn't born in a hospital. I have no social security number. My parents—"

"You have no parents."

That stung.

"Not anymore, but there has to be some record. Maybe if you tried facial recognition. My father used to say I was a clone of my mother."

He shook his head. I got the impression he had put my picture into a database. The results were disturbing him in some way.

"You're saying all traces of my parents have been wiped away," I said slowly.

He shook his head again. It didn't seem like a no, it seemed like he just didn't know.

"My uncle doesn't exist either, does he?"

"He's real. On paper."

"You don't sound convinced."

He shrugged. He smelled it on him. I could tell. Now would have been the time to joke about my uncle wearing super-villain cologne, but none of this was funny. "You felt something's off about him."

"I felt him trying to break the bones in my hand."

"What happens now?"

"Nothing."

"What do you mean nothing? Can't you do another search? I know you don't have a Spyscanner 3000, but you were using a special database, weren't you? What about DNA?"

"I can't," he said in a clipped tone.

"What are you saying?"

"I'm not *saying* anything."

"That's pretty obvious!" Had he stressed the word *saying*? Was he trying to tell me something without speaking? I studied his profile. He was tapping the steering wheel. I had taught myself Morse code, but he wasn't sending me any message I could decipher.

"Are we doing one for yes, two for no?"

He tapped the steering wheel twice.

"Was that a joke?"

Two taps.

"You want to be able to deny this conversation ever happened."

One tap. Yes.

"Did something come up in your search you're not telling me about?" I asked.

Two taps.

"Is someone telling you to stop searching?"

One quick beat on the steering wheel. My heart stopped beating altogether.

"That has to mean something."

No tap at all. He didn't know.

"Maybe it means you've hit on something sensitive, maybe someone's erased my parents as damage control."

His finger hovered over the steering wheel.

"They don't want me to find out what happened to my parents."

A hesitation, then two taps. He didn't think so.

"Maybe they don't want someone finding me."

No answer. A possibility?

"My uncle knows where I am obviously. Does he work for them?"

Two adamant taps. No.

I stared down the street at my uncle's house. Everything had changed. Nothing had changed. Axel had just basically admitted there was a *they*, without saying a word. And *they* were not going to help me.

I felt like a child claiming there was a monster under the bed. Someone had looked under the bed and confirmed it. My uncle's room was directly below mine. He was the monster under my bed. I had never slept well since I came to ██████████. This wasn't going to help.

My heart was palpitating. It wasn't Morse code, but I got the message: panic. I tried to take deep breaths. It only made me wonder how many of those breaths I might have left.

I saw my uncle leave the house.

"What's he doing?" Axel asked, straightening in his seat. My uncle had pulled an old-fashioned handkerchief from his pocket. It looked like he was polishing the doorknob.

"I told you, he wipes the prints off everything he touches."

He turned and looked directly at Axel's car. I couldn't see him smile from that distance, but I felt it like a cold draft.

We watched him walk in the opposite direction. When he disappeared around the corner, Axel opened the car door.

"Where are you going?"

"Why don't you give me a tour."

"My uncle doesn't like visitors. He's going to kill me." I wasn't joking.

Axel wouldn't be dissuaded from searching my uncle's house. He wasn't the one who had to live there. Or potentially die there.

The house was as quiet as a crypt with as much personality. There were no photographs on the walls, just furniture with hard edges and no character.

"Let's start with your room. Where is it?"

"I don't think that's necessary," I said, but my eyes showed him the way up the stairs.

"Do you want a minute to clean it up?"

"It's not that," I said as I followed him to the second floor.

I liked to be organized. Mrs. Hawkins told me it was because I needed to feel like I had some control over my life. She would have written that in my file, if she could have found it in the mountain of folders on her desk. She could have benefitted from some control issues herself.

Axel came to a doorway, reached inside, felt for the switch and flipped on the light. "Is this it?"

"Yes."

"Are you sure?"

I tried to see it through his eyes. My room was like any seventeen-year-old girl's room, except without all the makeup, the posters, the passionate diaries or the pictures of besties on a corkboard making funny faces. It looked completely unlived in. To be fair I couldn't say I'd really been living since I'd arrived in ████████.

Without asking, Axel opened my closet. You know how Einstein had seven suits that were all the same, so he didn't have to think about what to wear? The difference between me and Einstein is I was a lot more comfortable. My wardrobe consisted of multiples of exactly what I was wearing that day: sweats, tank top, and hoodie. Axel gave his head a shake.

He closed the closet, crossed the room to my desk, where he went through the drawers with nimble fingers. It didn't take long; I don't keep knickknacks.

I didn't have a computer. If I needed information, I used the school's outdated computer lab. I didn't like the idea of anyone spying on me at home through a device. My uncle was bad enough, but at least he was "family."

There was a stack of books on my desk. Axel ran a finger over the titles. They all had to do with survival. What to do if you were stranded in a jungle, a desert or on an island, etc. I hadn't managed to find a book about surviving a town like ████████. Maybe that's what I was trying to write with my dossier. On my nightstand was some pleasure reading: a handbook for medics, how to keep victims from bleeding out. The kind of stuff I wish I'd learned years ago.

The only other thing in the room was a bed with a gray comforter folded in a perfect rectangle on top. Axel turned to me with a look I'd come to recognize where he pursed his lips and raised his eyebrows, as if he were impressed.

Or maybe he thought I was crazy.

The other rooms on the second floor were completely empty. We went back to the ground floor where he went through my uncle's room. It looked as unlived-in as mine.

"You're not going to find anything. My uncle seemed pretty confident when he left the house. He looked at us to make sure we saw him."

And we didn't find a thing, until we got to the finished basement.

My uncle kept his stamp collection in custom-made cabinets with thin drawers that pulled out to reveal the stamps laid out under glass. Axel ran his fingers along the surrounding walls. There were no closets, no hidden recesses. He pulled out drawers of stamps, only glancing at the contents. The third drawer he picked made him freeze.

"Holy ██████."

I went to his side. "What is it? A secret lever?"

He pointed to a block of stamps that looked like they'd been part of a whole sheet. Depicted on them was a blue biplane surrounded by a red field.

"Do you know what this is worth?"

I leaned in to take a closer look. I'd never been that near to him. I know Axel wasn't wearing secret agent cologne, but does adrenalin have a scent? He smelled like swashbuckling, rough seas, high-speed chases, wild horses, and wide-open spaces. Adventure.

I tried to concentrate on the stamps. They were the old type that had to be licked to stick to an envelope, which to me made them less valuable than the modern self-stick ones which were less trouble. I read the price printed on each one: twenty-four cents. There were eight of them. I did a quick calculation in my head. "$1.92."

"That's an inverted Jenny. It's a famous mistake. The plane is upside down. Only one sheet made it into circulation. Just one of those stamps alone could be worth a million dollars."

It made me mad enough to spit, which of course would have ruined the stamps if they hadn't been under glass. I couldn't believe my uncle had that kind of money to support his philately. He didn't give me an allowance. He had groceries delivered once a month. That's why I'd been living on white bread and a cheese-like substance for the last week. I had no savings, no college fund. Here, he was sitting on a block of eight inverted Jennys. It had to be his nest egg, because I really didn't think he was the type to keep a checking account at the local credit union.

I wondered if he'd miss just one Jenny out of that block. I was sure she could pay for four years of college. I was also sure if I took one of those stamps from my uncle, I wouldn't live to see freshman orientation.

Axel did some more searching, but there was nothing else to see, nothing to prove.

We walked back to his car. The night had turned cool, but I was sweating. I heard the ratchety noises of late summer insects. They seemed to be singing *uh-oh, uh-oh* over and over, like the chorus in a Greek tragedy. When we stopped at his car, the streetlight threw my shadow out in front of me like the chalk outline of a body lying on the pavement.

"What do you think?" I asked Axel.

"Your uncle is not what he says he is, or he's exactly what he says he is."

"He's never said what he is," I said, throwing my hands up. "What do I do now?"

"Nothing."

"You mean just keep going on like before, waiting for something to happen?"

"I don't know what else to tell you, Talya. I don't know how to help you. That's not why I'm here."

"You believe me, don't you? That I don't belong here?"

He frowned. His hands were resting on the hood of the car.

His fingers tapped once for yes, twice for no.

"You don't not believe me," I guessed.

"I've got to go. I shouldn't have come in the first place."

I turned my head. I saw my uncle at the door. He waved. To any onlooker it would have looked like a hello. To me it was a warning, like the flag on a pirate ship, a skull and crossbones rippling peacefully in a soft wind.

Axel saw him too. He tapped the car like he was thinking. Like he was arguing with himself. One tap, a double tap, one, two.

He ducked into his car, reached into the glove compartment, and came out with a phone. He punched some buttons then handed it to me. "Here. This is a burner phone. I programmed in my number. Call me if something happens."

"Like, if he kills me."

"He's not going to kill you."

"You know that for sure?"

"I'll keep an eye on you while I'm here. That's all I can do."

An eye wasn't going to be enough. Not by a long shot.

"You're not always going to be here."

"No, I'm not." He looked down the road as if he could imagine himself already gone.

"Then teach me how to protect myself."

He shook his head. "I've read your dossier. You're smart. You're observant. You'll be okay." He didn't even notice he had tapped the hood of his car twice, until I looked pointedly at his fingers.

"Smart isn't enough. My head and a sharp pencil aren't weapons. You've got to give me something more. Teach me to fight."

He looked at me hard. I stared back. I didn't blink. He closed his eyes briefly as if imagining all the things that could go wrong. He sighed. "Tell me I am not going to regret this."

"You are not going to regret this," I swore. I put my hand over my heart. I didn't know it could turn out to be a lie.

Part of me hopes Axel regrets giving me the skills and know-how that led to a lot of hurt. That would mean he's still alive. Dead men have no regrets.

"We'll use the workout room in school. The custodian should be gone by now." He opened the car door. I reached for the handle on the passenger's side, but it was locked.

"I'll meet you there," he said.

"You're not going to take me?"

"I didn't say this would be easy."

He never told me *I* wouldn't regret it.

I followed his taillights until he turned the corner, and I kept running. Someday I'd see the last of him. I didn't want to think about that.

I'd been running the three miles to school since I arrived in ██████. Some athletes put sacks of flour in their backpacks. I never needed that. I was used to carrying fifty pounds of textbooks. Running without the burden of knowledge, I arrived at the school not at all winded.

I climbed the chain-link fence at the entrance to the stadium. I ignored the surveillance camera. It was fake. All the money in the school budget had gone to state-of-the-art mounted cameras to capture every angle of the football field during games. The cameras were stored in the state-of-the-art media center/AV room in the basement where a special journalism class edited the footage to broadcast the football games to the school's TV station. The class was supposed to serve the whole school, but it was basically a football adoration club, its members differentiated from the cheerleading club solely by the fact they didn't all wear skirts.

Ironically, the state of the arts had allowed the whole basement level to be turned into a state-of-the-art facility dedicated to football. All of the art rooms, the studio, the kilns, and all the music rooms not devoted to the marching band had been replaced by a new weight and workout room, the media center, and a locker room for the team.

On the opposite side of the hallway, the old rifle range hadn't been touched. It was a dank cinderblock dungeon with a sand berm at one end and beat-up gun lockers on the other. I knew it well. I had joined the rifle team when I came to ███████, because it was the only way I could get close to a firearm.

The hallway ran the length of the school, ending in a tunnel with direct access for the team to the inside of the stadium. It was closed off with a gate and a padlock. I picked the lock, let myself in, and closed it behind me. There was no sign of Axel. The lights were off in the workout room. The door was unlocked.

As soon as I crossed the threshold, the lights came on and two arms came around me from behind, one around my rib-cage, the other my throat. Both keeping me from breathing. Both like steel bars.

"Always be aware," Axel said against my ear. "Always have a plan."

I raised my foot to stamp on his toes, and he wrapped a leg around mine.

"And a plan B, and a plan C," he added. "Come on, Talya, what are you going to do?" The walls of the workout room were lined with mirrors. I didn't know what I was going to do. From the looks of my reflection, she was going to vomit and black out, not necessarily in that order.

Breathless. Sweating. Locked in Axel's embrace. I knew she'd imagined it, but not like this.

"What's your plan B?" he asked. I stared at my reflection to see if she had any ideas, but my vision was getting grainy along the edges, and she was slowly disintegrating. I didn't have the same option. I would just have to get used to not breathing.

"Damn it, Talya! You've got this lithe, supple body. Use it to your advantage."

I wasn't used to compliments. Lithe. Supple. They hit my heart like a one-two punch. It skipped a beat and made my knees buckle. My bodyweight and gravity tag-teamed to pull Axel off balance. He let me go.

I collapsed onto the mat, gagging and choking.

He leaned over me, biting his lip, his eyes serious. "Are you sure this is really what you want?"

I still couldn't speak. I nodded.

If this were a movie, the first beats of a thundering soundtrack would have started in that moment, as a training montage filled the screen. You'd see me gradually get stronger, faster, better, more popular, wearing better clothes, and no longer being afraid to eat lunch in the cafeteria. It would skip the plateaus and the pain.

This wasn't a movie.

Record Group No. 4

I didn't know exactly why Axel had come to ██████████. After a while I came to think he didn't know exactly why he'd come to ██████████ either. He was watching and waiting while helping me get strong. We fell into a routine. Routines can lull one into a false sense of security. Because nothing had happened didn't mean nothing would.

When something finally did happen, I didn't recognize it. It's hard to write about this now. Because Axel had been right. I observed everything, but I didn't really see what was in front of me. It's also painful to write this because two of my knuckles are broken. Maybe three, it's hard to tell with the swelling.

I have no idea how long I've been in this cell exactly. How long I've gone without medical attention. I can't tell the guards apart. They all have the same cold eyes, hard jaws, and buzzcuts. The men and the women. I notice the shift changes by the fresh uniforms. I don't know what the intervals are between them. Eight hours or ten or twelve? There is no natural light here. The fluorescents come on at odd times, usually just as soon as I've closed my eyes. I've been here three shifts so far.

They keep asking me how long my statement is going to take. Mr. Ebert always told us word count is our ruler not our dictator. I refuse to let them rush me. I learned the hard way to never ever leave anything out.

I won't go into every sparring session I had with Axel. I landed on the mats a million times. I got up a million and one. In the beginning Axel was probably thinking (and hoping) that I would quit. I didn't have that luxury. I had lost everything in the carjacking, except my life. I really wanted to hang onto it.

After a time, I think he started to enjoy our sessions. Not so much knocking me down (I hope), but the challenge of it.

He was as bored as I was in █████, and I was an eager student. Our routine was simple. We would find each other after dark on the football field. Axel would watch the surveillance video on his phone while I sprinted up and down the bleachers. We would go to the workout room and lift weights, then finally dance around the mats, sparring until Axel grew tired of it.

He didn't tire easily. I was fighting him and exhaustion. I needed to get into college. That meant I was still doing homework, filling out applications, and writing essays.

We went on like this for five weeks. If it had been basic training, I would have been past the halfway point. It was now the second week in October. One night, Axel didn't show up for our session. I didn't run the bleachers, I didn't lift weights. I propped the door to the workout room open a crack so I could hear him coming. I turned the lights off, lay down on the mats, and caught up on some rest.

Footsteps in the hall woke me. I didn't know what time it was, but I knew without even looking it was Mr. Reynolds. He had a back as straight as a washboard and a chest you could pin a medal on. The army had pinned many medals on him: for bravery, for courage under fire, for marksmanship, and other things he never let anyone close enough to read.

In return, he'd given more than his share, literally an arm and a leg. When he wore his prosthetics, you couldn't notice it from a distance, just a slight limp. I heard the almost imperceptible lag in his step.

He was coming out of the communications room. It wasn't completely surprising. He was the advisor for the media club. But it had to be after midnight.

He must have been speaking on his cell phone because I heard no one else in the hallway. "Just let me talk to her," he said. It was more like begging. Reynolds wasn't the begging kind.

"Tell her—" His voice broke, and he had to start again. "Tell her that I'm sorry. I know I let her down. I would do anything to get her back. Just let me talk to her. Please."

He wore a ring on his left hand, his only hand, so I knew he was married. I'd heard the rumors that his wife had left him suddenly, not even packing her clothes. I assumed he was speaking to his mother-in-law that night. Whoever it was, they didn't have much to say.

"Don't hang up on me, please," he begged. They must have ended the call, because I heard a crash, like his phone was being thrown against the concrete wall. The sound was followed by a string of the most creative curses I'd ever heard. Reynolds whispered a name I couldn't catch then said: "Forgive me. God forgive me."

I wondered what he'd done that had made both his wife and his God forsake him. I couldn't imagine a single thing. Not straight-laced, law and order, by-the book Reynolds. It never occurred to me to wonder what he might do in the future that would need forgiving.

I heard his lagging footsteps fade before I nodded off again.

I woke to Axel holding his hand out to me. He helped me up off the mat and in one continuous motion brought me down to it again. I was able to break the fall with my high cheekbone.

"Never let your guard down," he said.

I launched myself at him, striking with my fist, then elbow. He didn't even bother to block the blows. "That would hurt if you weren't pulling your punches. Punch like you're going through me."

I swung at him. He sidestepped, using my forward momentum to bring me to the mat again.

"Reynolds was here," I said, mostly to catch my breath. "I saw him coming out of the communications room."

"What was he doing in there?"

"I don't know, it's not like I can see through walls." I don't think Superman could have penetrated the communications room with his X-ray vision. I'd heard it had been built with layers of sound insulation and additional concrete. Reynolds could have set a bomb off in there and I wouldn't have heard it. I didn't mention his marital strife. I thought it was nobody's business but his own. I was wrong.

Maybe if Axel had been more forthcoming, I would have told him about Reynolds' phone conversation. I still didn't know why Axel was in [illegible]. I've learned a lot about interrogation techniques since I've been in this cell. Learning by doing or more specifically being done to. Back then the only skill I had was pestering. Like most forms of torture, it didn't yield the results I wanted. All I know is that after that night, Axel started to watch Reynolds more closely.

Axel didn't show up for chemistry class the next day. We'd sparred well into the night. I guessed he had the luxury of sleeping in and skipping first period.

I don't know why he never suspected Ms. Singleton, the chemistry teacher. She had enough knowledge and chemicals at her disposal to destroy the school if she wanted.

The chemistry room was a lot like this interrogation cell except bigger and with lab tables. It reeked of years of failed experiments. I couldn't tell how old Ms. Singleton was. I figured that working with kids, chemicals, and open flames could prematurely age a person. Her hair was streaked with gray. She wore it in a messy ponytail very similar to Ebert's. I noticed that because Ebert was there before class started. Ms. Singleton was flustered because all the digital scales had gone missing.

I picked a lab table close to the door, so I could hear their conversation.

"Do they have any ideas about who did it?" Ebert asked Ms. Singleton.

"No, but whoever it is, they're not using them to bake a cake. Those scales are accurate to 0.1 grams. Do you know how expensive they are?"

I didn't hear the rest of the conversation because Tommy came in and took a seat at my lab table.

"You look like [illegible]," he said conversationally.

I ignored him. He didn't seem to notice.

"You haven't gone into sleep mode since the new kid's been trying to get his hardware to interface with your software, huh?"

I looked away as Ms. Singleton threw a bag of marshmallows onto the lab table. Without the scales we couldn't do the lab she had planned, so instead we were going to create an exothermic chemical chain reaction. In other words, she was having us toast marshmallows to keep us busy.

I watched as she brought Ebert to the back of the room. She handed him something, but I didn't see what it was. I heard a whoosh that made me turn my head back to Tommy as he ignited the Bunsen burner with a lighter. At first, I thought he was going to set my hair on fire, but it didn't take me long to realize Tommy was serious about chemistry. I'm sure it had practical applications when it came to the future cooking his own meth. He could cut out the middleman. His eyes were focused, his hands steady. I thought he was a deadbeat, but I knew he was making a brisk trade in drugs. That meant he had a firm grip on economics and supply chain issues; he was a budding entrepreneur. Money was important to him. What was he willing to do for it? I needed to talk to Axel about Tommy being a suspect. But whatever Tommy might be capable of, I didn't think it would happen right then.

I turned to Singleton and Ebert. They were having an intense conversation I couldn't hear. At one point she touched his sleeve for emphasis. I didn't think they were talking about the missing scales anymore. Singleton was smiling. I'd never seen her do that before. She usually stood at the egress point (the classroom door) with her hand on the fire extinguisher when we did our labs. I realized that chemistry between people is real. You either have it or you don't. You could have all the baking soda in the world, but it takes just a little vinegar to make a science fair volcano.

On the other side of the room, I saw Darcy pop a marshmallow into her mouth and giggle. Chatham seemed annoyed, distracted from his calculations. I thought of oil and water.

Kamal was sitting with the girl who had smiled at me twice when I'd come to [illegible]. They were both quiet and studious, observing the marshmallows as they turned to charcoal. They bowed their heads toward each other as they wrote down their observations. Axel might think Kamal was learning chemistry with some ulterior motive, but Kamal was always a model student. He came from a place that respected education, teachers, and the metric system. Here, we only used metric for the important stuff, such as two-liter bottles of soda and grams of cocaine. I found that kind of funny.

I thought I was good at keeping my thoughts to myself. I must have smirked. Tommy popped the burnt offering of a marshmallow into his mouth, then put his hands under his chin. "Awww, are you dreaming about the new kid? Wait. Machines can't dream, can they? What were you doing, increasing capacity for his RAMS, if you know what I mean?"

"I have no idea what you mean," I made the mistake of saying. He clarified by making furtive gyrating motions that had nothing to do with Random Access Memory.

After chemistry, I met Axel on the way into English class. I pulled him aside. "Did you hear about the scales?"

He nodded.

"Tommy stole them," I whispered.

I was leaning against the lockers. He put a hand on them over my shoulder and put his head close to mine so no one else could hear us. "You saw him do it?"

"No, but maybe he's not satisfied with dealing drugs and wants to branch out into manufacturing. Can't you have him taken away?"

"You can't do away with someone just because you don't like him."

"It's not that I don't like him. I hate him."

Axel's eyes narrowed even further. "Is that a bruise?" He reached up and ran his thumb over my cheekbone. My eyes went wide, but he didn't notice. He was staring at my cheek. He frowned and cursed.

"You've got to stop breaking your fall with your face." His eyes moved over my features, maybe looking for other marks, before settling on my mouth. He shook himself as if he'd taken a sobering blow to his own face. "I've got to stop—"

I cut him off before his second thoughts took him away from my first thought. "I'm telling you it's Tommy who took the scales."

"Drugs aren't the only thing you'd need a scale for." Axel pushed away from the lockers, and I followed him into English class.

I stopped short. Axel saw what I did, a thick textbook lying on Ebert's desk: *Chemistry Basics: From Anthrax to Xanax*.

"Maybe he's doing research for a story," I whispered.

"A true story?" Axel asked.

We took our seats, and I imagined Axel rearranging his mental list of suspects.

I wasn't convinced Ebert was capable of violence. Part of me admired him, the way he kept showing up for class every day and coming back for more. Sure, I mean he got paid to do it. But there are some things you couldn't pay me to do. Teaching the kids at that high school was one of them.

He wrote *foreshadowing* on the board and drew lines emanating from it as if the word was exploding. Dark clouds were gathering on the horizon. They really were if you looked out of the classroom windows. It had been pleasant for too long; the weather was bound to change. I could tell by the dark looks on my classmates' faces the lesson was not going to go well. That was less foreshadowing and more precedent. None of Ebert's lessons went well.

The lights went off. Lightning must have hit a transformer somewhere. I watched Ebert's face go from light to dark. I shivered. He had prepared a presentation on mood and tone, but with the power out, he couldn't use it. He told us all to write a poem. Then he slumped into his chair and pulled out his cell phone, using the flashlight to see as he paged through the chemistry textbook. His face was lit from beneath, casting ghoulish shadows under his eyes.

I looked at Axel. I could see him fast-forwarding through security footage on his phone. He wasn't into literature, which was a shame, because he was the human embodiment of a poem, all graceful lines, fluid in his movements. And still a mystery to me, something I couldn't quite interpret. When I looked at him, something fluttered inside me, a trapped bird or a pinned butterfly. Sometimes when he looked at me, I saw something in his eyes that made me think he had some caged thing inside him, wanting to be free. Or was I seeing what I wanted to see?

Those thoughts would have made for a poem, but I couldn't corral them into verse. With the lights out, my head grew heavy. I closed my eyes just for a moment. I woke up at the end of the period, drooling on the unforgiving pillow of the desktop.

The power had come back on. I blinked into the harsh fluorescent light. I'd been dreaming I was flying in an inverted Jenny that was about to crash. Chatham was staring at me, his brow creased in a look of mild torment. Maybe he still hadn't figured out the difference between a paragraph and a free verse poem. I smiled at him in that unguarded moment, still half asleep. His mouth dropped open. I realized my glasses had come off, and he wasn't used to seeing me without them, or seeing me smile. I sat up straight, pushing my glasses back in place. He blinked and began writing feverishly. A break-through? Maybe it was that smile. Sometimes all a person needs is a little encouragement.

Mr. Ebert announced to the class that auditions for the school play would take place after school. He asked us to raise our hand if we would be showing up. I saw Axel square his shoulders and slowly raise his hand, like it was the last thing he wanted to do. Darcy's hand shot up an instant later like she'd been poked with a sharp stick.

My arm went up stiffly. It was a motion I wasn't used to. I had never once volunteered. I felt like I was raising a lightning rod into the stormy sky. Asking for trouble.

Axel turned to me, saw my raised hand, and sighed. If he wouldn't share information with me, and I couldn't beat it out of him, I had to stay as close to him as I could.

After class I went to my locker around the corner to put away my chemistry and English books and got out what I needed for civics. We had a few books for that class. One was called *My Rights*. Mr. Reynolds said it might as well be called *My Responsibilities* because no democracy could survive without an active citizenry. I cradled the books in one arm and stacked my dossier on top. I was about to close my locker when Chatham came up to me.

The hallway was emptying out. He stood there looking at me, biting his lip. I didn't often get this close to him. He was either with Darcy, or his entourage: Atkins, Carson, and Henderson usually flanked him on either side in the halls, forming an impenetrable line like they did on the football field. I'd been wanting to get him alone for a long time.

"I was wondering about homecoming," I began.

"Are you going to the dance? With Axel?"

"Axel doesn't dance." Actually, I didn't know that for sure. I thought about the way we sparred, how we moved in a kind of dance, striking, retreating, touching and coming away only to come back together again in new way. There was a rhythm to it, a soundtrack in our blows, an expelled breath, a groan.

I forced myself back to the present. Chatham's face was set. Maybe he was imagining a different type of dance, done horizontally. I cleared my throat.

"What's Kamal planning for homecoming?" I asked him bluntly.

"Kamal? He's been making a lot of calls home about it, that's all I know."

"If you hear these conversations, why don't you know?"

"He speaks in his language. The only word I understand is homecoming."

"Oh."

"Are you okay?"

"I'm fine, why?"

"How are things with Axel?"

"What do you mean?"

He looked at my cheek. "Is that a bruise?"

"Makeup." I never wore any. I threw the word out there, let him come to his own conclusions.

"I don't want you to get hurt."

I didn't want me getting hurt either. That's why I needed Axel.

"I can take care of myself." I was hoping that would one day soon be true.

He said he doubted it with his raised eyebrows. He didn't say anything with words.

He looked down and I noticed he was holding a piece of paper. He held it out to me.

"What's this?"

"A poem. For English class," he added quickly. Like I thought it would be for chemistry? Or for me?

I read through it quickly. It would have made a solid paragraph. For a poem it was bland. I knew it came from his heart.

It wasn't very memorable. I won't recite it here, except for two lines:

She puts up glass between my heart and hers.

See-through; can't break through. See me see you.

I pushed my glasses up, the lenses of which were technically polycarbonate plastic, not glass, by the way. I cleared my throat and looked at him. He was watching me closely.

"It's different," I said slowly.

He gave me a smile that curled protectively in on itself. He took the paper back, but I didn't let go. It tore over the word *heart* and ripped into two pieces.

"Thanks," he said, but his broad shoulders slumped as he began to walk away.

"You don't understand," I said to his retreating back. "Different is good. Different is awesome."

I don't know if he heard me. I was still holding a piece of his heart. I put the scrap of paper inside my dossier, thinking I could give it back to him at some point. I added the dossier to the stack of books in the crook of my elbow, closed my locker, and turned to find Darcy standing there.

I jumped and dropped all my books when I saw her. I wasn't scared of her. I just wasn't expecting her to be there. I was also wondering what she'd overheard or seen when I was talking to Chatham.

So, Darcy. Think of a cheerleader in your school, or THE cheerleader. Don't make a single change. Don't give her bigger pompoms, or heavier makeup, or a shorter skirt. She's exactly like you imagine her.

Her smile was brittle like it was made of hard plastic. "I don't know what he sees in you."

"I never—"

"You never what? Kissed a guy? Obvious. I really can't figure it out." She looked me up and down. I felt small, everywhere. "Is it your big frontal lobes? Do you do his homework for him? He's using you, you know. And you think I'm stupid."

"Chatham is not—"

She laughed. She glanced down at my dossier lying on the polished floor and gave it a kick. The scrap of paper with Chatham's poem fell out.

"You think you have everything and everyone figured out. I don't care about Chatham. I was talking about Axel." She put a sharp, manicured finger on my shoulder and gave me a push. "Keep your stubby fingernails off him."

I'm not proud of what I did next. I still can't tell you exactly why I did it. Because she had disrespected my dossier, my family heirloom and only friend? Because someone had to stand up for Chatham? Because she was making claims on Axel? All of the above?

I tapped her back, with all five of my stubby fingernails curled in against my palm. No matter that I thought cheerleading kept women on the sidelines literally and figuratively, I could no longer deny it was a real sport. Darcy was good at it. She did a cute sidestep as my fist hit locker 906 behind her. The number left an imprint on my knuckles. It's a good thing I was still pulling my punches, or I would have broken my hand. I know what that feels like now.

She flounced away, and I noticed she stepped on Chatham's *heart.* On paper at least. I picked up my dossier and carefully dusted it off. I opened it up and recorded my conversations with Chatham and with Darcy. I put the scrap of paper in as a bookmark. The hallway was completely empty. By now everyone else had gone on the fieldtrip to the zoo, or as the administration called it: lunch. I guess I should be grateful to Darcy. If she hadn't held me up at my locker, I would have missed what happened next.

Record Group No. 5

I picked up all my civics books and dossier and cradled them in my left arm. A few seconds later, I dropped them all again as I turned the corner and ran into my uncle.

"What are you doing here?" I asked.

"Parent-teacher conference."

I almost said, *You're not my parent*, but I needed something from him, desperately. I felt a pulse of hope that he was taking an interest in my education. "It's time to apply for financial aid. For college. And, um, to do that, we have to submit your tax forms."

"I guess you're not applying for financial aid then."

"You guess or you know?"

His mustache jerked upward on one side and a light came into his eyes. He leaned toward me, compressing my personal space. "If I were you, Talya, I wouldn't worry about the future at all."

I looked into his hard eyes. Maybe he meant I'd be coming into money as soon as I came of age. More probably I had no future at all. My knees went weak, and I dropped down to pick up my books. He kept on walking, not caring that he stepped directly on *My Rights*. It was just a book and just a title, but it made me shiver. Was that symbolism? Literal *and* figurative? Irony? Foreshadowing? The correct answer lately was turning out to be *all of the above*. I dusted off my books and dossier for a second time, put *My Rights* on top, and held on tight.

As I passed the library, I noticed the weekly newspaper lying in front of the locked door. I grabbed it with my free hand, let everything but the classifieds fall to the floor, and read through them on my way to the conference room. There it was—an announcement in the third column on the second page that told me I wouldn't live to see my eighteenth birthday.

I believed in rights and justice and other such ideas, but justice is blind and a lousy shot, and rights can't stop a bullet. I needed to be armed with more than just knowledge.

Axel looked up from his phone as I entered the conference room. "Where were you? I got this for you. You're not eating enough. It's cold by now."

He pushed a tray toward me. I'd heard the lunch choices on the announcements that morning. I knew it had to be Salisbury steak, but all I could see was dead meat. I had no appetite. I nodded. I was too upset to manage a *thanks*. I slid it out of my way to put the classified ads section of the newspaper on the table.

"My uncle was here, and he is going to kill me." I sank onto the seat next to Axel.

I swear Axel's hand flexed like he wanted to reach for a gun. "He's after you?"

"No, not yet. He said he was here for a parent-teacher conference."

"Which teacher?"

"I don't know. I ran into him by the library. He could have come from Ebert's room."

"Or Reynolds'. Your uncle actually said he wanted to kill you?"

"He told me I didn't need to worry about the future."

"That's not exactly a threat."

"Take a look at this." I pointed to the paper under job listings.

He leaned in and read the ad aloud: "Wanted: babysitter until end of year." There was nothing else, just a phone number with an unfamiliar area code.

He looked at me blankly. He shrugged.

"This is how my uncle's getting his instructions and his money."

"Talya—" Axel began, but he didn't seem to know what to say next.

"Try the number."

He sighed, tapped the number into his phone, and put it on speaker. I flinched at the screeching tone that came through before the automated message: "We're sorry. You have reached a number that is no longer in service or has been disconnected. Please check the number and dial again."

"It's a typo."

"I've read every edition of this paper since I came to [redacted]. It's appeared every six months. Always a different number. Always disconnected. Those are coordinates, not a telephone number. He goes to that location to pick up his money."

"That's not how coordinates work. There are too many digits in a telephone number."

"I've thought about that. Maybe the first two numbers show him what key to use to transcribe them."

Axel shook his head. "No one sends messages through the classifieds." He seemed to see something in my expression. He sighed. "Let me guess...your father—"

"One time he answered an ad to find a dog. He came back with a suitcase full of cash, looking like he'd been attacked by strays. I wanted him to get a rabies shot, but he told me the animal he had tracked down wasn't the kind who could give him rabies."

"You're sure your father wasn't a hitman?"

"Maybe he took the odd job here and there to make ends meet, but he had principles. He had training. He had that way about him."

"What about your mother?"

I sighed. He was trying to distract me. He should have known it was a tactic that never worked. "What about her?"

"Exactly. What about her? You never talk about her. It says a lot that you say so little."

I looked down. "I love her. I mean I loved her. I don't think I always saw her. She was like air. It keeps you alive, it gives you everything you need. It's always there. You don't notice it until it's gone, and you can't breathe." I cleared my throat and inhaled shakily. "She would have died for me. I know it. And I know my father would have killed for me. She was a complete pacifist. She didn't believe in guns. It's the only thing I ever heard them argue about." I looked up. "But I know guns are real and other people have them."

"You take after your father, I guess," Axel said. Maybe he was trying to lighten the mood.

"In philosophy maybe. He said I have her cheekbones. I look exactly like her when I smile." I caught a glimpse of my reflection, her lips in a tight line. She couldn't see the resemblance either. Maybe she, too, was forgetting what my mother looked like.

"I don't think I've ever seen you do that," Axel said softly.

"Do what?"

"Smile."

I shrugged. I looked down at the ad. "This one is different than the others that have appeared."

"How?"

"There's an end-date."

He glanced at the ad again. "What's so special about the end of the year?"

"I turn eighteen. Either my uncle's responsibilities end December 31st. Or I do."

Axel closed his eyes briefly and pinched the bridge of his nose like he had a headache or was trying to prevent one. "I think you're literally reading too much into this, Talya. How do you explain the upside down Jennys in your uncle's basement. You don't make that kind of money babysitting."

"Maybe he answers other ads. Like my father did, but for different reasons."

He nodded toward the paper. "Like for a handyman?"

"I checked that one out, it's legit. This one's new this week. *Vermin Problem: Exterminator needed through October 31st. URGENT. Many-pronged approach for complete eradication. Own equipment a must.*"

"It's getting cold. Rodents are looking for shelter."

"There are too many words, enough to hide a message in. What exterminator doesn't have equipment?"

"Halloween?"

"Which is also homecoming. It conflicts this year, so they're putting off trick or treating." That's how important football was. Scary, right? I'd hate to think what would happen if homecoming was held in late December. Wouldn't be much of a contest. A baby in a manger vs. a linebacker? Who do you think would come out on top?

Axel locked eyes with me. I thought he might believe me, but he shook his head.

"Call the number," I said in almost a whisper.

He did. The three shrill tones echoed off the walls in the small room. "'Check the number and try again.'"

We stared at each other. Was he as spooked as I was?

"No one reads the paper anymore, Talya," he said slowly.

"My uncle has it delivered. Paper is making a comeback."

"Not here it's not. This whole edition is like six pages. They don't even have a digital version."

"Exactly! Computers can be hacked. Paper can't be. It's ideal for the spy business. No one would see a message except if they knew to look for it."

"You don't know for sure this ad is meant for him."

"I don't know for sure it's not. You've got to help me."

"What do you think I'm doing every night with you. Against my better judgement."

"That takes time. He's got years of training. I've got weeks. He's got one hundred pounds on me and experience. There are ways of protecting myself where all I need is one finger." I held up my trigger finger.

"I am not going to put a gun in your hand."

"I already have one. I've been on the rifle team since I got to . Practice starts in a couple weeks."

"Then you don't need me."

"We shoot prone position with single bolt-action rifles. That's never going to help me. I need real training."

He shook his head as he got up to leave.

He tapped his trigger finger on the wanted section. "Stop worrying, Talya. This ad is not what you think it is."

"You'd bet your life on it?"

"Yes, I would."

"But you're not, are you? You're betting mine."

Mr. Reynolds was late to civics, so I had plenty of time to think about how little time I had left on this earth. To imagine Reynolds' classroom, think of this block cell. Don't change a thing except to add small desks with uncomfortable orange plastic chairs attached. Sitting in his class was kind of like being in solitary, but with twenty-seven other prisoners. To make up for the lack of windows, historical timelines had been plastered up like wallpaper.

People say history repeats itself. I studied the timelines on the wall as if they could tell me what was going to happen. Judging from past performance it would be nothing good. In the front above the board was the violent formation of the earth and brutal ancient history. Modern history started with the Thirty Years War in the far-right corner of the room and went through conflict after conflict. The timelines were one broad band of torment; in other words, high school in two dimensions.

Here and there was a bright spot like women's suffrage, but even Susan B. Anthony seemed to be saying with her frown that she didn't hold out much hope for mankind in general or womankind specifically. She seemed to be looking with one eye at Darcy by the door and with another at Tommy who was sleeping with his head resting against the wall and a depiction of the moon landing. I think he was drooling on Armstrong's fat space boot. One small step for man, I thought as I watched him. One giant waste of space.

I took my seat all the way in the front to the right next to Kamal on one side, who never noticed me, and Genghis Khan on the wall, who always stared at me with a murderous scowl. Someone had drawn a mustache on him, despite the fact he already had one. It made him look a lot like my uncle.

Axel sat behind me. The French Revolution was unfolding above his head on the timeline. Darcy seemed to have developed a keen interest in French history since his arrival. And I thought up new uses for pitchforks.

By the time Reynolds arrived, spit balls were flying like shrapnel, and two kids on the other side of the room had each other in a headlock. Either Reynolds didn't notice or care. He never said a word. His appearance was enough to cause order to break out of the chaos. He had always been trim, now he looked gaunt. I chalked it up to marital strife. He didn't look at us. His eyes roamed over the timeline as if he, too, was looking for future answers based on past performance. He didn't seem to find any. His eyes dropped and he gave a start as if just noticing we were there.

He picked up the remote control. I thought I saw his hand tremble as he clicked a button to project an image onto the whiteboard. The image of a man appeared instantly on the screen. A boy, really, with a bloody nose and black eyes. Reynolds stared at the face for a long time. He wiped his forehead with the back of his hand. He wasn't wearing his prosthetic arm.

When he clicked the pointer, a text appeared beneath it. *Name: ████████, aged seventeen, admits to killing thirty civilians in a terrorist attack. Under enhanced interrogation, gives information about the whereabouts of top ████████ operatives. Country: ████████, Date: 2014.*

"Seems reasonable, doesn't it?" Reynolds asked.

He paused. Silence stretched on longer than the Mesozoic era above the board. A rhetorical question isn't a question at all. It's a statement masquerading as a question. An answer is not expected and never given. When were the teachers going to realize that all questions in this school were rhetorical? Tommy was still fast asleep. The rest of the students were doodling or staring out the window or too chicken to put a hand up. Reynolds looked at me. I nodded.

A new image replaced the boy, a drawing of a young woman. Her face all eyes. Her eyes all fear. Another text: *Hildegard Lindenberger aged twenty-five admits to causing boils to form on a neighbor's cow and flying to the top of the mountain to take part in an orgy. Salzburg, Austria 1692.*

"Seem reasonable?" Reynolds asked again.

"Orgy?" Tommy raised his head. "What'd I miss?"

"What do these two people have in common?" Reynolds asked.

The silence dragged on.

"Black eyes," I finally whispered to put us all out of our suffering.

"That's right. Torture. Does it work?" He let the question hang there by its thumbs. Finally, I think he realized he wouldn't get an answer out of the class unless he beat it out of us. He looked around like he was seriously considering it before he went on.

"Torture doesn't get you the truth. It gets you what you want to hear." He went back to the first slide and stared into the scared eyes of that boy on screen. "This *confession* spawned an operation that cost the lives of three men and left six wounded. Do you know what they found?"

He rubbed the stump of his right arm with his left hand. No one dared venture a guess. I had a suspicion one of those wounded men was Reynolds. "They found a [redacted] goat." That kind of language would get a kid suspended and a teacher fired. Reynolds wasn't the kind of teacher you squealed on.

"The real operative was thirty miles away planting an IED that took more lives." His voice broke. He pointed out of habit with his right hand that didn't exist anymore, so he was really waving his stump at the board. "This kid wouldn't have known an operative from his rear end."

He looked around the class. "Torture simply does not work. It erodes the fabric of a civilized nation. We are not barbarians or inquisitors, or witch hunters. A confession obtained under duress is a lie and an injustice."

Tommy yawned. "I have a confession to make—I hate this class," he muttered under his breath. Mr. Reynolds put his good hand on his desk and hung his head and stared at the blank surface. I bet he was wondering if torture was really such a bad thing after all.

I looked back at Tommy. He was drawing a very phallic-looking rocket on the moon on the timeline. I was disappointed that Reynolds didn't send him to the moon for real. The teachers in our school seemed to have all agreed that ignoring Tommy was the only way to deal with him. I wished I could do that too, or at least be paid to do it.

"How would you get a confession at all without persuasion?" Kamal asked. By persuasion I had the idea he meant heated metal pokers and thumbscrews.

Reynolds looked up. "There's always another way. Sleep deprivation, psychological manipulation, planting a seed of doubt, making them question their own sanity. Drugs."

Those all left their own kind of mark, I thought. Of course, I didn't say that out loud.

He went on. "Sometimes it's just rapport, connecting with a subject on a very human level. Motivation is everything. Unless you're talking about a rare psychopath, most people's motivations are simple. If you know what makes a person tick, you can turn that against them." He turned his eyes again to the timeline on the wall, the section that featured the French Revolution. "A lot of times it's hatred. Sometimes it's hunger. Sometimes it's that burning desire for freedom." His voice softened. "Sometimes it's love."

"All that takes patience. What if you run out of time?" Kamal asked.

"I don't know." Reynolds rubbed his forehead with his good hand. "I just don't know." He wasn't talking to Kamal anymore. He was staring at Napoleon. I wondered what he was really seeing.

It started to rain then. There were no windows, and we couldn't see it. It beat against the flat roof of the school like hands against the drums of war. The screen went into sleep mode while Reynolds stood there staring at the blankness, his hand a fist, even after the bell rang.

Axel and I were the last to leave the classroom. We stood outside the door. "Reynolds has got some issues," Axel said in a low voice.

"Can you blame him?"

"No. But loss can make a man pretty bitter."

"Loss can make anyone bitter." Yeah, I heard some bitterness in my voice. "But Reynolds is straight as an arrow. He teaches civics. He's a decorated veteran. You heard him, he doesn't believe in torture."

"He's your favorite teacher," Axel said.

"What does that mean?"

"That maybe you can't see who he really is. Maybe he was the one having that parent-teacher conference with your uncle."

"I really don't think so."

"Why don't you ask him?" Axel said as he walked away.

I lingered at the door trying to summon up the courage.

I was about to take a step back into Reynolds' room when his cell phone rang. It must have been a new one, because I was pretty sure he'd thrown one against the concrete wall in the school's basement. "Let me talk to her," Reynolds said. "I will do anything to get her back."

I opened my dossier and flipped through the pages to the conversation I'd overheard when I thought he'd been talking to his mother-in-law. The conversations were exactly the same, except back then he had said he *would* do anything. *Will* was more definite, more immediate. And his tone was different. No longer begging. He wasn't talking to family. Maybe his wife had a boyfriend.

"When I have her back, I will hunt you down you son of a and I will strangle you with your own intestines, after I..." I won't repeat what he said next. It was graphic and disturbing. It made me think maybe he did believe in torture after all.

I never got up the courage to ask if he'd met with my uncle.

Record Group No. 6

We had tryouts for the play after school on the stage in the auditorium. We all sat on metal folding chairs. Darcy was upstage, but she kept turning around to throw poisonous glances my way. She should have been happy, she got what she wanted: the role of Juliet. I knew she wanted the role of Axel's girlfriend just as badly.

I wonder if she knew Juliet kills herself in *Romeo and Juliet.* This production was a mashup musical of Shakespeare's greatest hits from *Hamlet* to *The Taming of the Shrew*, so it left that important part out. It was an absolute tragedy.

It could have been worse. Axel was offered the role of Romeo, but he turned it down, saying he wanted to be part of the tech crew. A nominal part. Basically, so he could come and go as he pleased and keep tabs on Mr. Ebert. Darcy/Juliet acted like she didn't care, but she was a terrible actor; it was obvious she did care. I wasn't asked to read for a part. I was as invisible as an understudy.

Axel offered to check the sound equipment backstage while the tryouts continued. I knew it was just an excuse to nose around. I followed him.

Did you know there is a play about Charlie Brown? Ebert had produced it before I arrived in ██████. I'd heard it had been about as two-dimensional as a comic but not as funny. The props were being repurposed. Lucy's lemonade stand had been turned into Juliet's balcony by stringing a black curtain in front of it. I was leaning against it, watching Axel unscrew the back panel of a soundboard. I still didn't know what he was looking for. A bomb? It would be the perfect place to hide something attached to wires.

Backstage is like a back alley. There are all kinds of mysterious nooks, where illicit things could be done in the dark. I'd heard that during rehearsals last year, the Beast had gotten Beauty pregnant behind the scenes. Right then it seemed to be a pop-up market for illegal substances. From the corner of my eye, I saw shadowy figures emerge from a recess closer to the stage. There were only two places they could go. Out onto the stage itself where tryouts were still taking place, or down the side stairs where the controls were for the lights. One of them skulked away down the stairs. The other was Tommy.

"Hey, Watson," he said. He didn't mean Sherlock Holmes' sidekick. He was talking about IBM's artificial intelligence computer. He glanced over meaningfully at Axel who was pulling wires out of the back of the sound system. "Looks like your boyfriend's encoding someone else's motherboard if you know what I mean. You jealous?"

When I didn't say anything, he went on in a mechanical voice: "I am not programmed for emotion. What is jealousy? Does not compute."

Axel never looked up from what he was doing. In a low voice, he said: "I'll reprogram your whole system, Tommy, if you don't leave her alone."

Tommy slunk back into the shadows from whence he came. I barely noticed. I didn't need Axel to protect me. I was stronger than I'd ever been. I was pretty sure I could take Tommy, especially with his reflexes dulled by copious amounts of downers. But if you had no one in the world and someone stood up for you, you'd get a funny feeling that might feel a little like a drug. Or a lot like a drug.

I leaned my head against the frame of Juliet's balcony. I must have nodded off, because I never saw Axel put the panel back on the sound system. He was standing in front of me, touching my shoulder.

"Why don't you go home and get some rest. Take the night off."

I shook my head. He sighed and leaned toward me, putting

his hand on the flat desk-like surface of the balcony where the curtain ended.

"Are you even capable of nodding?"

I shook my head again, and he laughed softly.

He put his other hand under my chin. "It's not hard. You bring your head up like this." He raised my face to his. "Next, you simply give in to gravity and…" His voice trailed off, like he'd forgotten his lines. It was poorly lit backstage. His eyes were dark orbs. I couldn't say for sure exactly where they were focused, but my lips tingled.

We stood there silently, as if we were waiting for a cue. I could hear kids on stage reading from the script, the back and forth, the stilted lines. I was caught up in my own private drama. More like suspense. Maybe Axel did care about me. Maybe this wasn't a lonely one-sided soliloquy.

"That way madness lies!" King Lear exclaimed from the stage. Or the kid trying out for the role.

He was right. Love wasn't in the script or the stars. But our story wasn't finished. We were writing it as we went along.

Our heads were tilted toward each other, our lips close. I felt the sweet whisper of his breath, the heat from his body. He was closing the distance between us, bowing to gravity or some other force he was tired of fighting.

Just then the curtain behind us shivered. A robotic voice came softly from behind it. "Romeo, Romeo, wherefore art thou coordinates, Romeo?"

Axel straightened, moved away from me and put his fist through the curtain. There was nothing robotic about the howl that came echoing back. It sounded very human. It sounded very much like Tommy.

Revenge really is sweet, but what could have happened between Axel and me, could have been so much sweeter. What Tommy did was wrong on so many levels. In that famous quote, Juliet isn't asking where Romeo is, she's asking why he is. Why is he a Montague, someone she can't love. She and Romeo were from feuding families. Axel and I were from different worlds.

The lights went up backstage. Axel and I both blinked. He flexed his hand, the one he'd hit Tommy with. We both noticed a powder fall from it like a light snow.

Axel pushed the curtain aside and, there, where he'd been resting his hand on the board was a fine scattering of white dust.

"I bet it came off Tommy's nose when you hit him," I said.

"I doubt it."

"What is it?"

"I have no idea."

"Can't you taste it?"

He stared at me. "Yeah, sure. If I want to die."

"Can you collect enough of it to send to your people?"

"Go home, Talya."

"I don't have a home."

He sighed. "Go to your uncle's house. Nothing is going to happen."

He was right, only because I wasn't going to go home.

I left the auditorium. The school was mostly empty, only the custodian was still making his rounds. I couldn't go to my old supply closet where I used to eat lunch by myself. The custodian might need to access it. Besides it would feel like solitary confinement. (Or what I thought solitary confinement would feel like. Now I know what it's like for real. That supply closet in comparison was like a luxury suite.)

I made my way to the basement level, and I let myself in to the rifle range. Practice hadn't started up yet. It was cold, dank, and dark. Half the fluorescent lights in the ceiling were either out or going out, flickering like the lights in this interrogation cell, except here, it's a torture technique. In ████████ it was purely a budgetary issue. The school put more money into the mock rifles for the football team's color guard than it did into the whole rifle program.

The team was a small group of future accountants and computer programmers. It was, after all, the only sport you could do lying down. Except wrestling, but that required upper body strength, sweating, oh, and touching people. With Axel, I had all that and more. I'd outgrown the team. But if Axel wouldn't train me in small arms fire, I had to go back to what I knew.

I took the padlock off the gun locker I had used the previous year. I took out the 22-caliber single-bolt-action rifle with the heavy wooden stock. It wasn't pretty or new, but it was dependable and extremely satisfying to fire. It was like having an extra arm…that could kill someone.

I hadn't fired it in a long time and knew the sights were probably off by a hair. During practice we'd wear thick dusty jackets and wrap a brace around our arm and the stock for extra stability. I didn't bother with those, but I did put on some ear protection. I missed having Coach Aldrich behind me at the table. He would look downrange at the targets through a scope as we fired and tell us to adjust the sights a click left or right. It took a while for me to sight the rifle in on my own.

Insert a bullet, ratchet the bolt handle forward. Lock it down. Take off the safety. Hold my breath, ease the trigger back, fire. *Clickity-clack. Boom.* Safety on. Ratchet the bolt handle up and back to eject the empty shell casing. *Click. Clack.* Lay the gun down, get up, walk fifty feet, check the target, walk back, lay down. Repeat. The time-consuming part was resting after walking back and forth to get my heart rate back to normal.

Coach Aldrich had always stressed being calm before a match. He wouldn't even let us drink a Coke because of the caffeine, anything that might give us a buzz or a tremble. He told us not to look at the other competitors because a wink or a grimace on their part could raise our blood pressure, making us the slightest bit unsteady.

At the end of the range was a pile of sand which acted as a bullet stop. During the regular season, team members would have to dump buckets of water on it. I hadn't bothered. My bullets were sending up mini clouds of sand into the air. Eventually the clouds floated back to me and made me cough. Coughing initiates a change in intrathoracic pressure. Simply put, the pressure from the lungs affects the heart rate, pushing it higher.

So, when I finally had the gun sighted in and I fired a round through the bull's eye, I didn't jump up and down. I didn't pick up the rifle again. I turned the lights out, laid down on the mat and rested my eyes. I pulled the rifle close and felt safe for the first time in a long time. I drifted into a peaceful sleep. I had forgotten to take the ear protection off, so I never heard the heavy metal door of the range open from the hallway.

When I opened my eyes, I was staring into the deep, dark barrel of a 9mm.

I didn't react, at least outwardly. I didn't try to knock the gun away. I didn't scream. But inside my heart changed places with my stomach before it bounced back into place.

I took off my ear protection as Axel lowered the gun. "What the ██████ are you doing here, Talya?"

"Practicing."

"It looked like you were sleeping. I'm sure you'd be much more comfortable at home."

"I'm sure I'll stay much more alive here."

Axel blew out a breath. He raised the gun in my direction again, this time with the butt end toward me. "Here," he said curtly.

I scrambled up and took it from him. He was already having second thoughts as soon as it left his hand. I could tell by the tension in his shoulders and by the way he said: "I'm already having second thoughts about this."

I held the gun with two hands, pointing it down at the mat away from my feet. It felt heavy and blunt compared to my rifle.

"Don't be afraid of it."

"I'm not," I lied.

"Then what are you waiting for?"

"I woke up to a gun in the middle of my forehead. My blood pressure is sky high. Give me a second."

"No one is ever going to give you a second. You'll be lucky if you get a split second." He pushed my arm up. "Fire."

The target passed through my line of vision. I pulled the trigger. Nothing happened.

Axel swore under his breath, grabbed the gun, took the safety off, and handed it back to me.

I aimed again and fired. The target trembled as the bullet whizzed by. I gripped the gun harder, squeezed off another round and another. They left the target unscathed, but the sand pile took them all, exuding puffs, like it was sighing. I wasn't used to holding a gun like this. I'd always had an elbow on the mat.

Axel stepped behind me, adjusted my posture, nudged my feet into the proper stance with his toe. His chest was against my back. His arm was like a guard rail along mine.

"It's got to feel right, and natural."

I'm sure he was talking about my stance. All I could think about was the feel of him along the length of me.

"Steady and true," he said against my ear. I could hardly hear him over my own blood pounding.

If you ever wonder how biathletes do it, how they can cross-country ski then stop and hit a bull's eye when their heart is going a mile a minute, I can tell you what their secret is. They are robots. Every one of them. As I've made clear, I am not a robot.

I pulled off the last round and missed the sandpit entirely. The bullet ricocheted like a pinball before embedding itself in the concrete behind us.

Axel didn't move; I jumped a mile high. He swore, took the gun from me, and reloaded it.

"You've got to get out of your body. Out of your head. Go to a place of peace. Close your eyes."

I did. He started talking softly. I never would have believed it. He took me to a place of serenity. There was a tranquil mountain pool there of emerald blue. A sky disturbed only by the ripple of a soft white cloud. My heartbeat became one with the gentle rhythm of waves against the shore. In my mind, I lay down in the tall grass.

That peaceful place exploded suddenly in gunfire. The only scrap of the daydream that remained true was that I was really lying on the floor now. My hand went to my chest. My ribcage ached like I'd been shot through the heart. Axel finished unloading the clip on the target then looked down at me curled up in the fetal position.

He shook his head, shoved the pistol into his waistband, and sighed. No matter how hard I tried, I could not find my way back to that peaceful place.

Record Group No. 7

Another week went by since Axel had added small arms training to my regimen. I was spending more time with him, and even less time at my uncle's house. That meant less time sleeping. Axel seemed to need very little sleep. I was working up quite a deficit.

We faced each other on the mat. It was past midnight, but the workout room in the high school was middle-of-the-day bright, the fluorescents ricocheting off the wall-to-wall mirrors.

"You look awful," Axel said to me.

I glanced at my reflection over his shoulder. She looked hurt. And awful. The dark pools under her eyes had become flood plains.

"It's not a crime to say uncle," he said.

I straightened up. "He's exactly why I'm here."

I struck out at Axel. He blocked me, turned me, and took me down to the mat. I struggled for a minute before going limp. He sighed, removed his knee from my kidney and sat back as I rolled over sucking in air.

"Playing possum is not a plan, you know."

"Possums are not actually playing," I said, as soon as I was capable of speech. "Scientists say they actually collapse from shock."

"You think too much. Act!"

I sat up and made as if I was wiping sweat from my brow, but I let my backhand continue. He pushed it away. "Stop telegraphing everything. I can read every single thought on your face."

"What am I thinking now?"

"That you want my heart. You want to rip it out and wear it around your neck."

He was only partly right.

I pulled my fist back and aimed. "You're going to try a one-two punch," he said.

He was wrong. It was going to be a one-two-three punch. I never managed to count very high with him. I made it to 2.5 and he blocked them all. With one single jab, he knocked me to the mat again.

I telegraphed exactly what I was thinking, which can't be repeated here.

I rolled over and stood up. I did a back kick. He caught my foot, flipped it up, and I went into a graceless cartwheel. I came back swinging. He met me blocking. Each strike hurt more. I wasn't swinging any harder, in fact I was losing steam. Meanwhile, he was getting more frustrated, repelling me with more force. I landed again in a heap.

"Don't pull your punches." He reached down to help me up and in one smooth motion pulled me off balance. "Watch your center of gravity," he said after my center of gravity lay sprawled on the mat.

I knew from the motivational posters in Mr. Ebert's class that you just had to GET UP ONE MORE TIME THAN YOU FELL DOWN. It was not as easy as it sounded.

I kept going at Axel, each time with less control, leaving myself more open. He made a noise that was a groan, a growl, and a silent scream all in one. He took hold of my head like it was a basketball that he was about to crush. His fingers cupped the back of my head. His thumbs dug into my cheeks, just shy of the corners of my mouth. When he spoke, it was through gritted teeth.

"You're holding back."

Is that what he thought? I had nothing left to give.

"Give up?" He searched my eyes. I closed them.

"I can't afford to." The words hardly made it past my clenched jaw. "They told me I was lucky when my parents were killed. If that shot had been just an inch higher, I would have died. I don't want to be lucky. I want to be prepared. I have to be."

He didn't say anything. I opened my eyes. He was still cradling my skull in his hands like Hamlet and Yorick, except I was alive. He was staring at my mouth. I opened it slightly, but I don't remember now what I was going to say. His eyes met mine and he let me go like his fingers had been scalded. I'd been letting him hold me up and I sank to the mat and sat there stunned.

"You need a break," he said.

"No! I don't."

"I need a break." He ran a hand through his hair back and forth like he was erasing something inside his brain, some image or thought.

He turned away, but I could still see him in the mirror. "Don't you have a college essay to write anyway?"

"I'm not going to college."

His reflection looked angry. Axel turned and looked down on me. "You're too smart to not go to college."

"I can't apply for financial aid. Mrs. Hawkins says I'm not socially intelligent enough to get a scholarship. They want well-rounded individuals. I have good grades and I'm on the rifle team. She says they'll turn me down because I fit a certain profile. They think I'll shoot up a school."

"That's ridiculous." To his credit, and my discredit, neither of us saw that coming.

I shrugged. "Do I need a degree? Do I need to even finish high school? Would your people take me when I turn eighteen?"

He had never admitted to me he was an agent. It was an unspoken secret between us. The 9mm in his waistband was no longer secret, just another indicator. He no longer denied he had "people."

"You don't want what they have to offer. You can be anything."

"You sound like one of Mr. Ebert's motivational posters.

REACH FOR THE STARS, BUT DON'T FLY TOO CLOSE TO THE SUN."

"The sun is a star, isn't it? So, what does that even mean?"

I know he was trying to change the subject.

"Ask Tommy," I said.

"Why?"

"No one on earth would ever hire him."

He laughed. It was slightly contagious. The corners of my mouth eased upwards.

I guess he'd never seen that happen before. His own mouth dropped open. "You should smile more often."

I frowned. "You're just like Mrs. Hawkins." I took on her squeaky voice. "'You'd be pretty if you smiled more, or if you got contacts, or if you wore makeup, or if you stopped dressing like a boy or a gym rat, or a boy gym rat.'"

"Mrs. Hawkins is an idiot. You're beautiful just like you are. I just wish you could be happy."

I stared at him.

He sighed. "You think leaving school before you graduate is going to make you happy, but you're wrong."

Is that what he thought I was thinking at the moment? He had called me beautiful. The compliment was still ricocheting around my heart. I almost didn't hear what he said next.

"Trust me, you don't want this kind of life."

"You don't know what I want."

We glared at each other. The compliment he gave me was forgotten. Being beautiful was nice, being strong was preferable.

"You can't stop me," I said.

"Actually, I can."

"So, you wouldn't recommend me."

He shook his head.

"You don't think I can do it."

"I don't want you to. I want you to have a normal life. Marry Chatham. Have enough kids to form a football team."

"I don't want normal. Can't you see that?"

"What can I say to convince you?"

"Nothing," I replied.

He looked at me hard, like he was trying to see inside my head. He didn't understand me. Maybe he never would.

He tilted his head, and his eyes narrowed. "Then I'll show you why you don't want this. I'll give you a taste of what's in store for you if you go down that road. You're going to hate me, but someday you're going to thank me."

Axel kept me up for two days straight. It was still only half as long as what Navy Seals go through in training, but it was plenty for me. It was well after midnight, so we were into the early hours of Saturday morning. That meant I couldn't even catch up on sleep during school. He got in his car and followed me while I followed my shadow made by his headlights in the dark. At first my shadow ran with good form, straight posture, controlled arms, even steps. Over time she started to hunch over. After a couple hours, she loped along like a wounded animal. Finally, as the day opened an eyelid on the horizon, my shadow stopped running and puked. I stopped as well to give her time to recover.

Axel pulled to the curb. My shadow was already fading in the dawn. She evaporated completely as he switched off his headlights. I was fading myself but didn't have the luxury of disappearing. He got out, standing behind the open door.

"Give up?" he called to me. I could hear the hopeful note in his voice.

He still didn't know me. I wiped my mouth, shook my head, and ran some more. We ended up back at the school. The sun had risen. The world had taken on its hard edges again.

We went down to the range. He put on ear protection and napped, while I fired his 9mm until I couldn't hold it up anymore.

When Axel was rested, we sparred, right there in the range on the mats meant for shooters lying prone. I would have given anything to lie down. My fists felt like they weighed twenty pounds each. By the time we were done, I felt like I was pushing my hands through thick mud.

"Give up?" Axel asked after he'd knocked me to the mat for the umpteenth time. Lack of sleep is proven to diminish cognitive skills, motor skills, and things like place-keeping. I could no longer count. I didn't have any energy left for talking or shaking my head. I pushed myself up. Gravity had the consistency of quicksand.

I swung at Axel like I was swatting a fly. My own momentum would have taken me down if he hadn't caught me in a hold that felt awfully like a hug. I gave in to it.

"Forget what you see in the movies about torture. You don't need high-tech gadgets and secret lairs. Low-tech is just as effective. Maybe more so. There are so many ways of obtaining information." He started a list. "Sleep deprivation, light deprivation…"

I slept through the rest of what he was saying. "Hey." He shook me, then put both hands on either side of my head. "If you're exhausted enough, you'll admit to anything and everything."

I had a beautiful extended hallucination in which I admitted to him all the things I would do with him in the light deprivation.

"Do you give up, Talya?"

He may have thought I was nodding, but I had fallen asleep again briefly and my chin bounced down almost to my breastbone.

"Just give up," he whispered against my ear.

"No," I managed. He stared down at me. He wouldn't back down. I couldn't give up. There ensued a silence that was not at all awkward, because I slept through it.

By the afternoon, Axel said he had to go take care of some things. The football team had a game that night, and he needed to leave before they came.

He programmed the phone he had given me so that I had to access it every five minutes and type in the words: "Be careful what you wish for." The deal was, if I missed a check-in, I lost and would give up. I had a life to lose, if this didn't work out.

I didn't say I didn't cheat. I used the same phone to set myself an alarm to ring half a minute before check-in. It took me longer to type those words in as time went on. I got less sleep than I thought. Maybe two minutes tops. It was better than nothing.

Axel came back to the range that night. We did some things I won't admit to even under enhanced interrogation, except it was all a hallucination brought on by sleep deprivation. I did not consider that part torture.

I hadn't had anything to eat or drink since Friday at lunch. I got so thirsty I even considered using the water fountain outside the range at the end of the hallway. I checked the phone. Its clock was set to military time. I saw four zeros in a row. My cognitive function was pretty impaired by that time. Had we counted down to the end of the world? I was too tired to get upset if we had. It took me a whole minute (to when the display changed to 00:01) to figure out that it was midnight.

I went out into the hallway and stumbled my way to the water fountain. The spicket looked like a stalagmite, encrusted with years of calcium deposits, saliva, and germs. I pushed the lever to produce a thin waterfall of brownish liquid. It smelled like sulfur and tasted like rust. It was delicious. I drank for 3.5 minutes until my alarm rang. I checked in, typing faster now, the water having refreshed me like a drooping daisy.

That's when Kamal came in from the stadium entrance into the hall.

He looked right at me, but he didn't notice me. It was a talent the rich and the privileged have of not seeing the rest of us unless they need something. Even then, they don't really know who we are. We are waitstaff and cleaners, cashiers and cogs.

He was dressed in a suit, that I'm pretty sure was tailored.

That meant he hadn't suited up to play but had to be present for the game. Maybe he'd stayed out on the field dreaming of what it would be like to be the starting quarterback.

He was speaking into his phone. I didn't understand the language, but I knew anger when I heard it. He switched to English. "They're going to regret it if they don't do what I ask. They're going to lose everything!"

I went back to the range, trying to remember what he said, so I could write it in my dossier. Something about regretting to ask someone something who lost something. By the time my phone's alarm rang again, I forgot what had been said and who had said it.

When Axel came back for real, late Sunday morning, he looked like he hadn't slept well. It still seemed like a luxury compared to not having slept at all.

"Let's go for a run," he said glumly.

He followed me in his car, past the football stadium, through treelined streets. We were into the third week in October. It was a warm day. A fluke. One last soft touch before the cold bore down for real. I didn't know how much more I could take, but I couldn't stop. I had to prove myself. I had everything to lose.

We passed the convenience store on the outskirts of town. Axel put his blinker on and turned in. I stopped running and doubled over with my hands on my knees. I saw him get out to put gas in the car. I started running with a renewed sense of urgency right into the woods.

I moved as silently through the underbrush as I could, stopping every few moments to listen for footsteps. Most great discoveries happen by accident. I tripped over a downed tree that was half rotted. With some effort I kicked out as much of the rot as I could.

I was able to create a hollow just big enough for me to fit in. I had taken off my hoodie when I was running. It wasn't completely soaked with sweat, just the arms where they'd been tied around my waist. I didn't plan to stay there long. I wasn't worried about night and hypothermia. I should have been.

I don't know what time it was when I woke up. It was dark and noisy. We think of nature as peaceful and quiet, but there's a surprising amount of rustling going on and flapping.

The moon was out. When my eyes adjusted to the dark, I sat up and gathered the leaves that were in arm's length to cover myself for an added layer of insulation. At one point my hand touched something furry, but it skittered away before it could take a bite of me. Or before I could take a bite of it. I would have been tempted, if I had a campfire.

I tried to think happy thoughts. I tried to remember details of my family's adventures. All I could think of was: if they could only see me now! If they could, they probably would have cried. For the record I didn't cry. I didn't have enough liquid in me to waste.

Record Group No. 8

Anyone who says they sleep well under a blanket of stars, probably also slept under a real blanket. I didn't think I had slept at all, but I must have dozed here and there, because a beam of sun was on me like an interrogation lamp. I didn't want to see the light. I rolled over and the leaves crinkled around me. I could smell the earth, the decay, the rotting log. It was a pretty low point. Maybe not my lowest ever (carjacking, remember?). When you're down that far, a couple inches in either direction doesn't seem to make that much of a difference.

A crow had awoken me. It was pecking at my little finger, thinking probably it was a worm. Which is about how I felt. I could see it was a crow by its straight beak. I would have preferred a raven. At least there was something poetic about them. If they poke your eyes out, maybe you'll be memorialized in some ode where the word *Nevermore* undulates throughout the centuries. To be pecked at by your average garden-variety crow? It's simply humiliating.

I turned over and it flapped away, croaking at me from its eternal sore throat. That put me back under the interrogation lamp of the sun. The questions came at me, and they wouldn't stop. I blinked under the harsh light. *What are you thinking? Is this worth it? Who do you think you are? What do you hope to accomplish? You seriously think you will ever find out in a million years what happened to your parents? You think Axel will ever love you back?*

I didn't say a word. I had no answers.

I pulled twigs out of my hair all the way to my uncle's house. I was out of the woods, not in the clear. When I opened the door, my uncle was about to descend into the basement like a beast into its lair. I was heading up the stairs, but his iron gaze was enough to stop me. "You're spending a lot of time with the new kid," he said. "What do you two talk about?"

"We don't do much talking." I realized how that sounded. I turned red. I was about to say, *It's not what you think*, but I didn't want him to think about what Axel and I were really doing. As I stood there, a leaf fell from my hair. He watched it fall.

"I didn't sign up for this," he said.

I had? I'd love to see the application for that. Two dead parents, please, and hold the friends. And give me one distant relative (in every definition of distant), who scares the out of me. I guess it could have been worse. Maybe I was still on the waitlist for two evil stepsisters.

"Don't worry, I'm being careful," I said into the awkward silence. Maybe he thought I meant I wouldn't get pregnant. That he wouldn't have to take care of two dependents. I meant I was taking measures to protect myself from him.

He shrugged. "What do I care? You're not going to be my responsibility much longer." He started whistling as he went down the stairs.

I wasn't cold, but I shivered.

Upstairs in the bathroom mirror my reflection looked like a scarecrow. There was a dried stalk of something I pulled out of her hair. She was too tired to thank me. I couldn't tell where the dark circles under her eyes started, and dirt began.

I took a quick shower, afraid I'd fall into a microsleep and drown. A microsleep is exactly what it sounds like. When you've had too little rest, you fall asleep for a split second. It happens to pilots after long flights, which can lead to them crashing onto the runway. It happens to drivers all the time, causing them to drift into the oncoming lane and crash. You're probably seeing a trend here. Crashing and burning.

I wanted to crawl into bed, but I thought about the monster under it, in the basement, poring over his stamp collection, maybe plotting ways to get rid of me. Besides, Axel might find me there. It was safer in school.

If Ebert or Kamal or Reynolds gave up any clues, I wouldn't know. I slept through all my classes.

At the end of the day, I went to my locker. I couldn't remember the combination. I rested my head against the cold metal, trying to think.

I don't know how long I stood like that. Suddenly Axel was at my side, his lips at my ear. He said some wonderful things, then I woke up. He was still there, but a lot angrier.

"Where the hell have you been?" he asked in a harsh whisper.

"Getting some rest."

"At least one of us did. I was out looking for you all night." His tone was clipped.

"You didn't break me," I said proudly.

He ran a hand through his dark hair. I realized he wasn't angry with me, but with himself. "I've been pushing you too hard." He raised a hand to touch my cheek but dropped it before it reached me. His tone softened. "I forgot how young you are." He studied my features like he was memorizing them. Like he was remembering exactly how young I was, and that he wouldn't forget it again.

Axel hadn't broken me, but damage had been done to the fragile connection between us. It had developed a hairline fracture that I couldn't see. Because I didn't want to see it.

He refused to train with me for a few days. He said it was to give me time to recover. I think now he was putting time and space between us, already pushing me away.

By Thursday when we went back to our old routine, things weren't quite the same. I was stronger. Too much practice can lead to plateauing. He'd been right, I had needed a break. I was faster, had more endurance, but there was one thing I still couldn't get.

We threw hands for a while in the workout room under the school. But it wasn't long before Axel threw up his hands.

"You're still pulling every punch. Your technique is improving, you're gaining strength, but you're not following through."

He took my fist and brought it to his chest. "Don't end here. Make like you're going through me, then through the basement wall."

We sparred again. Basically, it was me tapping him, him blocking me and knocking me back until I was up against the mirrored wall.

"Why are you pulling your punches?" he yelled at me.

"I don't want to hurt you!"

He stared at me for a moment. Then he laughed until he started to cry.

"You aren't hurting me," he said when he could get his breath back. "You're killing me, if you know what I mean."

That phrase! *If you know what I mean.* I was staring at Axel, but all I saw was Tommy's ugly head. I was too close for a jab, so I hit the phantom Tommy with a roundhouse from the right. I followed up from the left. By that time Tommy's face had disappeared. Axel stumbled back, giving me some room to raise my knee to my chest. He must have still had tears in his eyes How else could he have allowed me to forward-kick him in the breastbone?

He stumbled back some more. I kept coming. I landed one more blow before he blocked me. That wasn't what made me stop. It was the blood trickling down his temple from under his hairline.

"Oh my gosh! Your head. It's bleeding. I am so sorry."

"Don't apologize," he said gruffly.

He had stopped laughing a while ago. He touched his thumb to the side of his face, pulled it away, and looked at the blood. I kind of noticed him turn his hand into a fist. I was more concerned with his bloody temple.

"I feel bad, I didn't mean—"

"You know what happens when you feel bad?"

He didn't give me a chance to answer. He put his fist into my solar plexus. It wasn't all that hard, it was more like an instructional tap, but I folded like a lawn chair. Except a lawn chair doesn't have to try with all its might not to vomit.

"You all right?" he bent down to ask me.

I wanted to respond. I really did, but you need air to speak.

"I'm sorry," he said, as he turned to the bench to get a towel like he usually did when our sessions were over.

"I thought you said never to apologize," I said, or at least I thought it. I lurched toward him. I was aiming for his broad shoulders. I managed to hit the back of his knee. He cursed and went down just barely on the mat.

He rose up in one smooth motion. I saw the surprise on his face, heard the respect in his voice. "Whatever you're channeling, keep doing it."

Who would have ever thought that Tommy could be good for something? By wanting to break through Tommy's skull, I'd made a breakthrough.

Punch through. Follow through. Always have a plan, never be distracted. These are the things Axel had taught me, and I'd internalized them. *Don't celebrate too early*, I learned the hard way as Axel came at me. I was busy patting myself on the back when he struck at me. I didn't block him with my hand. I used the side of my face. I didn't see stars unless you count Pluto as a star, which I guess a lot of people do. I dropped to my knees.

"Damn it!" Axel said, as he dropped down next to me. "Let me see it."

"It's fine," I lied.

"I hurt you."

"So that someone in the future won't hurt me more."

I got up, turning away from him, but my reflection showed him the red welt across my cheekbone and the way her one eye was partly shut like she was squinting. She looked unsteady. She fell back onto the mat.

Axel groaned like it had hurt him more than me. He took my head in both hands and tilted it up toward the light. He ran his thumb over my cheek, probing gently like a doctor would.

I sucked in a breath. His eyes went to my open mouth, back to my cheek and down again. Then he met my eyes. He looked tormented like I'd struck him somehow deep and true. When he let me go, I swayed. Not because he'd hit me. I was reacting to that piercing gaze.

He helped me up, put an arm around my waist, and walked me out to his car. I no longer needed the assistance, but I wasn't going to tell him not to touch me.

As he drove me home, I asked him to turn down the heavy metal.

"I'm not playing anything," he said in a tight voice. It was my head pounding, not his stereo. I was glad he'd disabled the dome light so he couldn't see how my cheek was swelling. I was going to have a nasty bruise. That was the least of my worries. That would fade. The more serious damage had been done to the connection we had. It already had a hairline crack. This was only helping to split it and us apart.

Record Group No. 9

I woke up with a headache the next morning. I wasn't surprised. I'd gone to bed with one. I kept my hair down and brushed it over my left eye. There were plenty of kids who wore it like that, boys and girls. Sometimes I wondered how they could see anything. Now I wondered what they were hiding.

I ran into Chatham at my locker. Seeing out of one eye, you lose some sense of depth perception. He put a hand on my upper arm to steady me, even though I wasn't wobbly.

"Your hair." He stared at it for a minute. "It's different."

"Gee, thanks." I tried to free my arm, but he held onto it.

"No, different is good." His eyes roamed over my hair and face.

"Different is awesome," he added. He gave me a smile. It was like getting a bright package that you couldn't wait to unwrap. I tilted my head to look at it, and the curtain of my hair moved.

"Is that a—" His voice trailed off before he said the word *bruise*. He reached out a hand, but pulled it back before he touched me.

I didn't answer, because he never finished the question. Everyone noticed it that day. No one wanted to talk about it directly.

Axel didn't show up for chemistry or English. I slept through both classes. When he saw me outside of the civics classroom, he looked pained, before he looked away.

Reynolds wasn't much of a smiler. That thin line of his lips got even tighter when I walked into class. He looked back and forth between Axel and me, then glared up at the picture of Susan B. Anthony on the timeline. He seemed to be finding it a shame the suffragettes had made so much progress for me to blow it all.

It was Friday. The next day, the football team was playing its last game before homecoming which was a little over a week away. Chatham wore his jersey. Darcy sat in front of him in her cheerleading uniform. It showed her shoulders, her midriff, and her knees in three violations of the dress code.

I didn't see anything wrong with any of those body parts. Personally, I never showed my midriff. If you had a scar from a bullet entrance wound, you probably wouldn't either. If other people wanted to show theirs (midriff, not scar), it was no concern of mine. What bothered me is that the dress code was applied unevenly. By that, I mean never applied to cheerleaders. Football was above the law in ██████. Give me a D. Give me an O and all the rest of the letters that spell double standard.

Reynolds hadn't moved on from the topic of torture. He was just going farther back in time. On the whiteboard, was a slide depicting various methods dating back to the Middle Ages. There were shaming parades. The pillory, two wooden planks hinged together with holes cut out for a person's head and hands. The scold's bridle, essentially a muzzle. Then there was the cucking chair that could be dipped into a body of water along with the body occupying it. These techniques could be for anybody, but they were reserved mostly for women who refused to act in a reserved manner.

Before Reynolds could move on to the next slide, Mrs. Hawkins came on the loudspeaker to lecture us about the importance of adhering to the dress code. I could hear the stones around her neck making *tsk, tsk* sounds. Darcy looked completely unconcerned.

A girl came into class as soon as the announcement ended. She wore a pink sweatshirt two sizes too small which made her breasts look abnormally large. There was a sequined unicorn on the front, and its horn was pointing at one of them. I kept notes on my classmates, remember? I knew that's not what she'd come to school wearing. She'd had on a skirt that kissed the top of her knees, a tank top with thin straps, and her usual kind, friendly smile. She'd shown me that smile twice when I'd first come to [redacted]. The outfit from the morning had disappeared, along with the smile. She was hiccupping as she took her seat next to Kamal.

Reynolds scowled at her. "We don't have pillories or scold's bridles or cucking chairs anymore, but how far have we come?"

I could tell Reynolds hadn't had hall or bathroom duty in a while. Since I came to [redacted], I'd seen kids pilloried in their lockers. I'd heard of a kid muzzled by his own jock strap in gym class. Had Reynolds truly never heard of a swirly, in which someone's head would be pushed into a flushing toilet? And shaming parades? For some kids that was the three-minute-long gauntlet through the hallways between classes. We hadn't come far at all since the Middle Ages.

Reynolds turned to the board and drew a big square. Painstakingly with his left hand, he wrote two words in the box. *Systemic Inequality*. He turned back to us.

"We don't put people in pillories; we put them in boxes. We sort and categorize and discriminate. We don't ignore differences, but sometimes we ignore people with differences." He held up his right arm. He wasn't wearing his prosthetic. "This makes me invisible," he said as some kids glanced away, or looked down at their desks.

"And sometimes we draw negative attention to differences. Did you know girls are five times more likely than boys to receive a dress code violation?" I did know that. I had written it in the paper I'd submitted for his class. "Do you know what the punishment is for a dress code violation in this school?" The girl who had come in late didn't say, but she let out a sob.

Reynolds went back to the board, erased *systemic inequality* and scrawled in *lost and found* in its place. "We may not do shaming parades anymore, but we parade people—mostly girls—through the school after making them put on clothes other people forget to bring home."

That sob from before, from two seats over? It turned into something longer that gave me shivers. I pulled my hoodie up over my bare shoulders. I'd never been written up, only because people (except Tommy who I don't consider a person) never noticed me. The girl two seats down got noticed, for the crime of simply growing into her body.

Reynolds looked at the unicorn emblazoned on her chest like a scarlet and sequined letter. If he fixed you with that kind of drill sergeant glare, you'd have trouble telling the difference between righteousness and anger. I can't tell you the kind of noise that girl made next because I'd never heard it before or since. Kamal took his football windbreaker off the back of his chair and handed it to her.

He was a real prince. I hoped Axel noticed that.

Maybe she had issues with dressing in general, because instead of putting her arms through the sleeves of Kamal's jacket, she put the whole thing over her head. It looked even more ridiculous than the unicorn, but at least it muffled that disturbing sound she was making.

"Look, it's a burka," Tommy sniggered from the back.

She got up and ran. I was hoping she'd find her way to the bathroom where she could cry in peace. I hoped she wouldn't go to Mrs. Hawkins who would probably tell her it was okay to believe in unicorns. Because of the windbreaker over her head, she didn't see the door frame and cracked into it on the way out.

"Oooh, that's gonna leave a mark," Tommy said.

I knew the bruise would fade. The emotional scar was going to last a lifetime. A rumble of laughter started. Reynolds killed it with an angry glare.

"How different is our dress code from a burka?" he asked.

Personally, I thought it was more a difference in yardage of fabric than it was in philosophy. I knew better than to say that out loud in [redacted].

Reynolds sighed into the quiet. "If you won't talk to me,

then discuss it with a partner." He began handing back the papers we'd written.

Great! Partner work. For me, it was right up there next to pillories when talking about punishment. Axel was checking surveillance footage on his phone. Kamal had lost his potential partner to the left. I turned to him, only because he was snapping his fingers as if he was trying to think of something.

"Taylor," he finally said.

"Talya," I muttered.

"In my kingdom, no one wears a burka." Did he mean *in my kingdom*, the way we would say *in my country*? He had that something about him that screamed privilege, wealth, and power that hadn't been earned. It wasn't just what he drove, the Mercedes in the school parking lot. It was the way he walked. He smelled like money.

"*No one* wears a burka?" I repeated. "I think what you meant to say is no woman wears a burka."

He waved my statement regally away. "I personally do not like the burka. I believe a woman's hair is one of her best attributes."

"You're funny."

"I'm not trying to be."

I thought his ideas about wimminfolk were pretty out of line, but here's something for comparison. We lived in a town where the cheerleaders had a designated football player (usually their boyfriend) for whom they baked cookies before every game. And they had the privilege of taking their player's sweaty jersey home after games to wash it.

I stared at Kamal. I wasn't sure what to say. I don't think he meant to be a misogynist. I really think he was just born that way. From the timeline I felt Susan B. Anthony's disgruntled gaze. "Do you know what I think is a woman's best attribute?" I asked Kamal.

"What?"

"Her right to vote."

He tilted his head. "You're funny," he said slowly, as if trying to decide if that was a good thing.

I tilted my head the other way. "Are women allowed to have a sense of humor in *your kingdom*?"

"Yes, of course. But only on weekends and certain holidays."

He smiled. It was a wide, self-satisfied grin, but also generous. Could bad guys be likeable? The bell rang before I could make up my mind.

I didn't leave civics right away. Mr. Reynolds was still handing back papers. It was a drawn-out process since he only had the one hand. Mine was the last one in the pile. He took Kamal's empty chair next to me. He looked past me, scowling at Genghis Khan on the wall. Across the centuries, Khan stared back.

"Do you know what I see when I look at this timeline?" he said (Reynolds not Khan). "A whole lot of bullies. And every once in a while, someone with the balls to stand up to them." His gaze went to Susan B. Anthony, who'd gotten us the right to vote. She had balls figuratively and thanks to some nameless, bored student who had doodled a pair, she had them literally too. "So much value, so much potential, so seldom used." I wasn't sure if he was talking about me, the student body, or the Susan B. Anthony dollar coin that's still in circulation, though you'd never know it.

He focused on me now. "Sometimes I think you're the only student in here. The only one who hears what I have to say. You can go places, if you don't let a bully stand in your way."

"Tommy—" I began, but he cut me off.

"I'm not talking about him."

He put my paper on my desk. His finger obscured the grade.

"I thought you were smarter than this."

"I know I haven't been putting enough time into my work," I stammered.

"I'm not talking about your grade. Even your worst effort is still miles ahead of everyone else's." He pushed my paper toward me. I'd gotten an A.

"Don't let Axel use you."

"Maybe I'm using him. Does anybody ever think of that?"

He made a noise expressing his disbelief: "Pfffft."

It sounded exactly like a bullet passing close to my ear. I know this now from experience.

"You're taking it out of context," I said.

"What's the context? You think he loves you? Let me tell you, I would do anything for love. Anything," he repeated. His voice seemed reinforced with steel and barbed wire. It made me shiver. "I would never do that." He pointed vaguely to the bruise under my eye.

"It's not what you're thinking."

He stood up and looked down at me. "You have no idea what I'm thinking."

From the way he glared, I had an inkling he was thinking of murder…and Axel.

Whatever the reason Reynolds' wife had left him, it wasn't because of abuse. I believed he wouldn't hurt someone he loved. But someone he had no love for? I needed to talk to Axel. I had study hall after civics. I'd been meeting Axel in the conference room next to Mrs. Hawkins' office instead. I considered it supplemental training. At that point he was teaching me about ballistics.

Firing a gun was as easy as pointing and shooting. Hitting an intended target was more complicated. There were factors to consider like wind drift, time of flight, bullet weight, even temperature. Axel had me doing some complex calculations based on a variety of conditions. Maybe he was just trying to keep me busy, to keep me from asking other questions. I don't think he ever intended for me to use the information. At that point it was purely theoretical, but it was going to have practical applications in my near future. I was learning just enough to be dangerous.

That day, I never made it to the conference room. Mrs. Hawkins was standing outside her office, waiting for me. The stones around her neck shuddered as she swung her arm motioning me inside.

We sat in silence interrupted only by the gurgling of her desktop fountain. It had turned into an underground stream beneath a mountain of folders. She stared at the purple circle under my eye for a long time. The minutes ticked by.

She believed it was an act of violence to drag things out of students. "Soooo," she said, stretching the word until I thought she was going to break its back. But she clearly had no appetite for torture. She gave in. "That looks painful."

"It is."

"You've been spending a lot of time with Axel."

"I tutor him. It was your idea."

"That's not what I'm talking about. Did he do this to you?"

"What?"

She couldn't bring herself to say it. She drew a circle with her finger around my face. "That. Did he?"

"Did he?" I echoed.

She leaned forward, clasping her hands together until her knuckles turned white. "Listen, Talya, some very smart people can make very stupid decisions." She closed her eyes for a moment and bit her lip. "I'm sorry. I apologize for using the s-word." She put both her hands out toward me as if she were stopping a car in traffic. The stones around her neck clinked together angrily. "I care about you, and I don't want to see you doing something you're going to regret."

I remained silent. The dismissal bell rang. She had kept me that long. She threw up her hands. "What would your mother say, Talya?"

I stood up. I said exactly what my mother would say. Nothing. The dead can't speak.

I met Axel outside the conference room door. "Reynolds looks like he wants to kill you," I warned him.

"He just came to see me. He told me as much."

"What did he say?"

"If I laid a hand on you again, he'd kill me."

"He could get fired for that," I said.

"I don't think he'd care."

"You think he would? Kill you, I mean."

"He could try."

"He could succeed. He's a sniper."

"Former."

"I'm sure it's like riding a bike. It comes back to you."

"He's disabled."

I shook my head. "He's underestimated."

"He's right."

"About what?"

"I hurt you."

"So that someone else won't! Can't you see that?"

He stared at me, like he was trying to see. "I've got to go," he said.

"I'll see you later?"

"I've got stuff to do. We're not practicing tonight."

"I'll see you tomorrow?"

"I can't."

I got the feeling it wasn't because he couldn't, but because he wouldn't.

I watched him walk away. Chatham was coming the other way. Neither of them moved to the side. Their shoulders collided, and it changed their trajectories. Chatham stopped when he reached me. I thought he was going to talk to me about the bruise, but something at the other end of the hallway caught his eye. His brow creased, and he smiled.

I turned to see what he was looking at. There must truly be something magical about unicorns. The girl from civics still had Kamal's varsity windbreaker and right then she had his hand in hers. If Kamal was planning something bad for homecoming, would having a girlfriend make him change his plans? Or was she simply a cover for him?

Record Group No. 10

We were supposed to have play practice six days a week, but Ebert had canceled for Saturday because of the football game. I had the feeling Axel would be in the auditorium anyway. I didn't know where else to find him. I didn't know where he lived. I never did find out. I'd tried to follow him a bunch of times. He'd always evaded me.

The stage was dark. I found Axel by following the gleam of the flashlight on his phone. He was kneeling in front of Juliet's balcony, running a hand over the wooden frame. I didn't know what he was looking for. I don't think he did either.

I approached so quietly he couldn't have heard me. "Go home, Talya," he said with a sigh without looking up.

"Not until you tell me why you won't practice with me."

"You need a break."

"No, I don't."

"Then I do. Damn it, Talya, don't you get it?" He pounded his fist on the floor.

"Get what?"

He made a shushing noise. He pounded on the floor again, but not angrily, more exploratorily. It sounded hollow.

He shoved the balcony back to reveal a trap door. He ran his hand along the outline of it until he found a latch and pulled it up. We had found the missing scales from Ms. Singelton's chemistry room. We could see them perfectly clearly, because at that moment the backstage lights clicked on.

I knew the controls were at the side steps. Whoever had turned on the lights wasn't supposed to be there either. Whoever it was might be headed for the trap door. Probably for nefarious purposes. Whoever it was would see us as soon as they hit the top step. I didn't have stage fright, but I froze. My eyes, however, darted about, trying to decide if we should exit stage left or right.

Axel shook his head as if he could read my mind. He put a finger to his lips. Gently he put the trap door back in place and stood up. What was his plan? Pretend to be statues, blend into the scenery? We were surrounded by scenery, but we were going to stick out like a sore thumb. As he took a quiet step closer to me, I realized he was going to blend in another way.

Axel cradled the back of my head in his palm like he was about to replay the famous scene in which Hamlet holds up an empty skull and says: "Alas, poor Yorick." But I felt more alive than ever. Axel closed the distance between us, bent his head to mine and hesitated as if he were waiting for a line, or waiting for the curtain to open, or wondering if this was really a good idea.

Was it an act what happened next? Maybe it started out that way. We'd been close before. We'd had our hands all over each other. In my defense, it was in learning to defend myself. Yeah, it made my heart race when he had me in a headlock or pinned against the mat, but my heart started beating a different kind of rhythm. Bordering on palpitation.

I knew I wasn't meant for this role, but like an understudy who finally gets a chance to shine, I was going to give it everything I had. He moved toward me. I was already meeting him halfway. We came together the way a collision sculpts two separate cars into a wreck in a burst of heat and steam. His fingers were in my hair. My arms were around his back, my fists grabbing handfuls of his ACDC shirt. I couldn't pull him close enough. I was pinned between his firm thighs and Juliet's balcony. But my heart was turning over and over like a car hurtling down a cliff. Right then, I couldn't tell the difference between flying and falling. It's the landing that makes all the difference.

We came to a jarring stop as Ebert pulled us apart, his hands like the jaws of life, except being separated felt like dying.

He pulled us to the stage door and pushed me out into the hallway. He didn't let Axel go.

I leaned against the cold concrete wall, shaking. There was not a mark on me, but like it sometimes happens in an accident, not a single one of my internal organs was where it was supposed to be.

I waited for Axel outside the stage door. It was torture, what I was feeling. Figuratively. As opposed to now, here, in this cell. The guards have changed shifts three more times since I've had something to eat or drink. I would tell them anything to get some relief. All I have is the truth. They don't seem to want that. They tell me Axel didn't care about me. You can lie about a lot of things. That kiss was telling the truth.

But it couldn't tell me what was going to happen next. How it would end. That kiss, that attack on my senses, happened against the backdrop of *Romeo and Juliet.* I don't have to tell you it's a tragedy.

When Axel finally came out, he sighed when he saw me. "Listen, Talya, about what happened in there—" he began. That kind of sentence never ends well.

"What did Ebert do to you?" I interrupted him.

"Do? He gave me a good talking to. Told me what a bastard I was for dragging a nice girl like you down to my level." He frowned down at my mouth. "He's right."

"Maybe I'm not as nice as he thinks." I tried to sound tough; it came out as a question.

He met my eyes. "Maybe I'm more of a bastard than he knows."

His eyes dropped to my mouth again. I stayed completely still, like you would if you're close to a rare, beautiful, wild creature you don't want to scare away. A somewhat dangerous creature that could devour you.

His phone vibrated. The ringer was off, but I could hear it, like it had been gagged and was trying to get our attention. He had never gotten a call that I was aware of. He looked down at the screen. His eyes narrowed. He didn't look at me.

"I've got to take this," he said. "I've got to go."

I didn't like the finality I heard. "You mean go for now, not for always," I said to his retreating back.

He didn't answer.

Record Group No. 11

Out of habit I went down to the school basement. Maybe I was hoping Axel would come back. I had forgotten all about the game. The hall was filled with football players coming and going. I turned to leave, but Chatham had already spotted me. He jogged over to where I stood at the end of the hallway.

"Hey," he said.

"Hey."

"You're coming to the game," he stated, with no hint of an inflection or question in his voice.

"Why not, I've got nothing else to do." His blue eyes seemed to turn bluer. His big shoulders sank.

"I mean, no, yeah, I'm really looking forward to it," I amended.

"I've got to go get ready. I'll throw a touchdown for you."

"No, really, I don't want you to go to any extra trouble."

"For you, I'd go through any amount of trouble." He turned back toward the locker room, leaving me standing there.

I didn't know what to say to that. I didn't know I'd be taking him up on that offer in the not-too-distant future. I don't know if he regrets it.

I sat in the bleachers half-way up at the 0-yard-line. We were well into autumn. The air had that crinkly smell of decay and change, of things ending.

As the players took the field, I saw Chatham look around in the crowd. It almost looked like he waved. To me. I glanced around to the left, to the right, then behind me. I didn't see anyone wave back. When I looked back again, Darcy and the rest of the cheerleaders were dancing and twirling their way onto the field. She gestured to me, but it wasn't a wave. It was a windy day. You don't have to torture me to get me to admit this: in my head, I was calculating how I would alter a shot to factor in drift and distance, if I were aiming for Darcy's pompom.

We all stood for the Anthem. Directly below me, I saw Reynolds on the sidelines with a couple of students from the media club. He put his only hand over his heart. It looked somewhat awkward, but completely sincere. Next to him was a state-of-the-art video camera, the kind you see on professional fields, mounted on a four-foot tripod that could swivel.

Across the stadium from where I sat was the press box, open to the air except for an overhang. A short wall separated it from the bleachers. Behind the students taking stats, the time was displayed in blood-red digital numbers.

Play started and stopped. I don't understand football. It seemed to be a lot of set-up, a whistle and everyone would be lying down on the field. When the players were standing, though, Chatham stood out. He was fast, he was agile, he was strong. He scored touchdown after touchdown. I didn't imagine they were all for me. I also don't think I imagined he looked up to the stands where I was sitting each time he scored.

He seemed to know where the ball was going to be. He didn't so much catch it as cradle it and protect it only to set it free and let it soar. It was obvious he loved the game. The game seemed to love him back. The opposing players on the other hand feared him. He was gentle and graceful, but he was brutal in his takedowns, flinging players to the ground one-handed like they were empty dummies.

It was thrilling to watch…in the three-minute increments when the ball was actually in play. Otherwise, I got pretty bored. My mind kept wandering back to Axel. To that kiss. To that phone call. To the image of his back turned to me. To kill the time, I imagined firing a gun from every angle of the stadium. My calculations were made incredibly easy by the yard markings on the field.

During half-time the marching band came out. I can't tell

you what song they played even under interrogation. It was beaten unrecognizable by the drum section. Part of the band was the color guard. They played no instruments at all. Some of them were twirling flags. I didn't like that the rest of them carried mock rifles. What if they weren't all mock? They looked like basic single-shot 22s, nothing automatic. Very much like the rifle I used in the range in the school basement. That made me feel better. Even if they were real, I thought, how much damage could a weapon like that do? Seriously.

The second half of the game was pretty much like the first, with more stops than starts, a few moments of exhilaration here and there, spread out along a continuum of boredom. I won't describe it in any more detail. You don't even need to know the score. Let me just say it was a complete massacre.

After the game, I let myself into the range. It seemed cavernous and hollow without Axel. I opened the gun locker and lifted out my rifle. I'd been neglecting it in favor of his 9mm. It was like getting together with an old friend who could kill someone. I picked up where we had left off.

I lay down on the mat, and fired one shot after another. Load, ratchet, fire, ratchet, expel, load again. I disengaged my mind, let muscle memory take over. I felt somewhat like a machine. I stopped when I'd emptied a box of ammunition.

When I went to check the target, I couldn't believe it. One of my shots had gone straight through the bull's eye. All the others had missed. I pulled the paper target from its clips and held it up to the flickering fluorescent light. The hole in the middle was too large for a single shot. I hadn't missed at all. Every shot had hit its mark, straight through the center.

I pinned up a fresh target before going back to the mats. Since the range had no natural ventilation, a fan had been built into the wall venting to the outside. It was so powerful, I'd seen it suck loose targets into the grate and anything else that wasn't literally nailed down. I turned it on, and got back down on the mats, this time accounting for wind velocity, firing a couple clicks to the left without adjusting my sights. I went through another box of ammo. I turned the fan off and checked my target. I had kept my glasses on for protection while firing. I took them off now to see more clearly.

The results were the same as before. Dead center.

I wanted to tell someone. That's not exactly the truth. I wanted to tell Axel. But he seemed to be avoiding me. I was preoccupied when I left the range. The game was long over. I didn't expect there to be any traffic in the hallway.

As soon as I stepped outside the range, I ran into Chatham.

It was a collision at low speed, but it threw me off balance. It made me wonder what it felt like when Chatham meant to hit somebody. His shoulders rose up like mountains under his padded jersey. He put two hands on my much smaller shoulders, to steady me. He didn't let me go. "Hey," he said.

"Hey."

"Did you get contacts?"

I realized I'd left my glasses in the range. I didn't say anything. I felt exposed, naked without them. The feeling wasn't as awkward as you'd imagine.

"Your eyes," he said. "They're the color of deerskin."

His own eyes were intense, focused and narrowed, like he was looking through the cross hairs of a scope. I blinked.

"That bruise—you never told me how you got it."

I wasn't going to go into it now. "Why are you still here? The game's been over for ages."

"I like to stay out on the field to go over the plays in my head with no one else around. Think about what worked, what didn't. Visualize what I could do better. What did you think about the game?" His voice sounded shy.

"I really don't understand it."

"You can ask me anything."

I really wasn't that interested, but I did have a question: "How do you get into the press box?"

"Through the men's locker room." He nodded toward the steel door. "There's another hallway and a stairwell at the end that leads directly to it."

"Doesn't that make it hard for women to get up there?"

"I never thought about it," he said. Neither did the designers. "Were you practicing? I didn't think rifle season started already." I didn't know he knew I was on the rifle team.

"I need to tell Coach Aldrich I'm quitting," I said, not answering his question, but also not lying.

Chatham drew me in closer and bent his head to look into my deerskin-colored eyes. I'd always known he had beautiful blue eyes himself. This close, I could see there were specks of gold in there too; a burning horizon touching a wheat field. A wheat field a deer could graze in—before it's shot.

"Can I ask why?"

"Why, what?" Between beautiful for spacious skies and amber waves of grain…and his strong hands on my shoulders, I'd gotten distracted.

"Why you're quitting the team?"

"Um, well, you know, we've got a lot of homework…"

"Can I talk to you for a minute?"

"Aren't we talking already?"

He didn't wait for an answer. His hands left my shoulders, only so he could take me by the elbow. He guided me into the workout room across the hall which was empty.

"Actually, I wanted to talk to you too. How are Kamal's plans going for homecoming?" I asked.

"I don't know. He still calls home a lot about it. He sounds frustrated. I'm not sure he's got the best relationship with his father."

"That's too bad." I thought about how he'd given his jacket to the girl in civics. "He's a real prince," I murmured.

Chatham tensed. Something struck me about his reaction. I just didn't know exactly what. He let me go, but he still held me with that wholesome wheaty gaze, which was very distracting.

"I'm concerned about you, Talya."

"About me?"

He nodded. "You don't tutor anymore. You're withdrawing from a favorite activity."

It sounded as if he was reading that off a brochure for a battered woman's shelter. I had an image of him, his mountainous shoulders hunched over the computer googling abusive relationships. Thinking of me.

I put a hand on the summit of his shoulder pad. It was so high up it was next to his ear. "Chatham, that's so sweet, but you don't have to worry about me."

He turned a light shade of red. "I'm not. I'm worried about Axel and how he's treating you. I'm not sure he's good for you." He straightened up and my hand slipped from the cliff of his shoulder. "In fact, I know he's not."

"Not what?" Axel said from the doorway. "What are you two talking about?"

"Calculus," I said glibly.

Chatham pushed me out of the way to stand in front of me. Gently of course, but I was still being sidelined. "Actually, I was telling her you're no good for her."

"Actually, she doesn't like to be told things," Axel said.

"You're using her," Chatham responded.

I stepped around him so that we formed a triangle. "Maybe I'm using him," I said. "Does anyone ever think of that?"

It was obvious they hadn't thought of it. They both gave a humorless laugh.

"Listen," I said to Chatham. "I appreciate your concern, it's really sweet, but I can take care of myself."

"No, you can't," they said at the same time.

I couldn't blame Chatham too much. He was born into this town where the girls danced on the sidelines and baked cookies for their heroes on the football field.

But Axel? I thought he knew me. He did know me! He didn't believe in me. I thought I'd convinced him, showed him how hard I could work, how I wouldn't give up. He still didn't see me. I thought of a poster in Mr. Ebert's room: CONFIDENCE IS NOT HAVING TO PROVE ANYTHING. Maybe I wasn't as confident as I thought, because I wanted to prove Axel wrong. So badly.

I clasped my hands together and brought them up to my cheek. "Oh my, whatever would a girl like me ever do without strong men like you?"

Hands still locked, I swung at Axel as hard as I could. He blocked it. Just. I was already grabbing a weight bar off a stand and swinging again. He blocked it with his forearm, but it had to hurt. I jump-kicked him. He avoided me, but I glanced his hip, and he went off balance. I came in with a one-two punch, except it was a one-two-three-four punch. I landed just a quarter of them. The math was good enough for me.

These had always been private battles between Axel and me. I almost forgot Chatham was there until Axel had me pinned, my back to his front, one hand holding my head against his shoulder, the other arm in a chokehold around my neck. I put both hands on his arm. He might have thought I was trying to ease the pressure. Instead, I was holding on like onto a chin-up bar, so I could lift my legs up. I was going to kick Axel in the head in a move I'd been saving.

But Chatham moved in at that moment, and I clipped him just under the chin, sending him flying into the mirror on the far wall. It didn't crack, but he was still going to have at least seven days of bad luck. I could tell by the sound his skull made, and by the way his eyes rolled back in his head that he had gotten a concussion.

Axel let me go. I ran to Chatham's side and helped him sit up. "Oh my gosh, Chatham, I am so sorry."

"What was that?" he said in a slow voice.

"My foot."

"No." He waved his hand vaguely in the air. "What was all that?"

Axel was kneeling on Chatham's other side. We exchanged

a look. Mine said: *what should we tell him*? His said: *beats me, you started this.*

"You're…" Chatham began then broke off. His eyes rolled back in his head before he focused on me again. "You're different. You're amazing."

Axel pulled Chatham to a standing position. "All right, let's get you back to the locker room."

I took his other arm, and we walked him over like a football hero. The locker room was like a shrine. Each player had a cubby with a light shining down on a life-sized poster of themselves. The benches were like altars. We laid Chatham down in front of his two-dimensional self. I looked into the blue eyes and said a prayer that the real Chatham would be okay.

I found his phone and texted his entourage to come take care of him. I held his hand for a minute. "Listen, Chatham, could you do me a favor? Don't tell anyone about this, okay?"

He shook his head and winced.

"Promise?" I asked.

"Promise."

I didn't know a ball had been set in motion. And I was the one who had kicked it into play by kicking Chatham under the chin. Everything that happened a week later at the homecoming game was my fault.

Outside the locker room, I leaned against the concrete block wall and took a deep breath. Axel stared off down the corridor.

"He's not going to say anything," I said to Axel. "And what if he does? People will know we work out together? He knows how things are around here. There's no way he could ever bring himself to say out loud that a girl knocked him out. They won't know why you're here." I blew out a breath. "I don't even know exactly why you're here."

All of a sudden, I did.

I thought of the way Chatham had tensed as if I'd struck him with the truth. What had I said? *Kamal is a real prince.* I'd meant he was a gentleman. It was literally true. "Kamal is a prince for real," I said. Axel tensed in the same way Chatham had. "That's why you're here. Not to watch him. To watch over him." I took a step toward him. He didn't deny or confirm it. He didn't say a word. "You're not a bodyguard, you're not with him enough. But there's a threat against him, isn't there? And you don't know where it's coming from."

"No," he said harshly. "You were right. Nothing has ever happened in [redacted]. Nothing ever will."

"You don't believe that."

He shrugged. "It doesn't matter what I believe. I'm being recalled." His eyes were still focused on the end of the hallway. He was already far away, already putting distance between us. Leaving me behind.

"What? Why?"

"I shouldn't be telling you this. It was a wild goose chase. There was a tip early on from some insider in a terrorist cell in some corner of the world. Nothing definite. Nothing since then."

"Maybe the informant was killed," I said slowly.

"Maybe they were making up information for money. Maybe the information was extracted by extraordinary measures and wasn't true."

"You're saying someone gave up false information under torture."

He shrugged. "There's nothing coming from this side. No sign that contact has been established, no phone traffic, no messages. Dead silence."

"What about the want ads in the newspaper?"

He blew out a breath. "You see what you want to see, Talya. Not what's in front of you."

"You know your people are wrong, don't you?"

He shrugged. "I've contacted someone I think I can trust. I also mentioned you."

"What did he say?"

"*She* hasn't said anything. I put it in a letter and mailed it."

He agreed with me. Paper was making a comeback. But it had its limitations.

"Do you know how badly funded the postal service is? They won't get it in time if they get it at all! You might as well put a message in a bottle and drop it in a puddle. When are you leaving?"

"The first of the month."

"You'll still be here for homecoming. We can—"

"*We* aren't going to do anything. This is my responsibility. I've let you get too close. That was obviously a mistake."

"If you mean what just happened with Chatham—"

"Chatham was right," Axel said softly. "I'm not good for you. I've been a complete idiot letting you in, getting you involved. If something happened to you…" He reached out and smoothed my hair away from my forehead to tuck it behind my ear, then brushed his knuckles along my jaw line. "I could never forgive myself," he whispered. He bent his head toward me, seemed to think better of it and straightened, his lips forming a tight fence. He put his hands on my shoulders and pushed me gently away. "This has to stop before I do something I regret." He looked at my mouth. He looked wistful.

"The dead don't have regrets. I want regrets. I don't want to just survive. I want to live. I was locked up in my own prison before you came. I am not going back to solitary!"

I didn't know what was in my future, that I'd make a lie of that. There were so many things I thought were true.

"I'm sorry, Talya. This is over."

This. There had been a *this*! I couldn't accept that *this* was turning to *nothing*.

"It's better this way."

"Why does everyone think they know what's good for me?"

I gave him more than enough time to respond as I stood there shaking with unexpressed feeling. He shrugged his shoulders. I expressed myself without saying a word. I let out all the hurt and fear and, yeah, anger. I went after him, not exactly like my life depended on it. Like my love depended on it.

I don't know what I was thinking. That if I could prove to him that I could hold my own, he'd let me back in? I stopped thinking at all. I wasn't exactly a machine. Machines don't have hearts that are breaking, but I reached a higher physical plane where thought and feeling are suspended and the purely physical takes over. Was it Zen-like? Like understanding the meaning of one hand clapping? No. It was my one hand attacking, the other blocking. Bone on bone. It was something desperate and beautiful. For a few moments that stretched out of time, we were united in a contest of wills that seemed violently choreographed, evenly matched. I couldn't sustain it. He had years, mass, and experience on me. Finally, I fell, dragging him down on top of me to the unforgiving concrete of the hallway.

"You're going to be the death of me," he said. (Please tell me that was not foreshadowing!) "Let's stop fighting." He was out of breath.

I nodded. I pulled his head down and I kissed him. That surprised him more than a punch. At first, he didn't do anything as I mashed my lips against his. Then he returned the kiss. I won't go into detail here. It's not something you can reconstruct blow by blow. It was like a battle but sweeter, two separate entities taking and giving, merging into one.

I have no idea how long that kiss lasted, but it wasn't long enough. He rolled off me onto the cold floor and sat there panting, looking at me like he'd lost a war.

"I won't do this to you," he said. "I care about you too much. This has to end before I do something I can't take back."

"What about me?"

"I'm trying to protect you!" Did he realize that protecting felt like murder?

I stood and looked down at him. "No one," I said in a hard voice, "is ever going to make a decision for me again. I get a say in this too. And *I* say it's over!"

Record Group No. 12

The next day was Sunday, so I didn't have school. I didn't have school Monday, Tuesday, Wednesday, and Thursday either. It was in session; I just didn't go. I didn't get out of bed for two days. I couldn't. Grief made gravity stronger. I had felt this way after my parents were killed. Except with Axel there was the added pain of knowing he was going on without me.

The thing about being human is that eventually hunger and thirst start to compete with heartache. They can never outweigh it, but self-preservation kicks in. You get back to the business of surviving, if not living.

When I finally crawled out of the fetal position, I felt like I'd been reborn. I had nothing to do except mountains of homework. I no longer cared about that. Without a scholarship or financial aid, I couldn't afford to go to college. I had no future. At least that's what it felt like. I didn't know yet it would turn out to be true.

I tried not to think too far ahead. I concentrated on the moment. And at that moment I felt powerful. I slept during the day. At night I ran the bleachers by myself. I let myself into the school basement. I lifted weights. I shadow-boxed with my reflection. She looked angry and sad, but I had to admire her form. I could barely keep up with her.

By Friday I was back in school. It was the last day before homecoming. I felt I had to be there. All the scales had reappeared in the chemistry room. I knew where they'd been. I didn't volunteer that information.

In English, Ebert was trying to explain the difference between the climax of a story and the denouement. Climax was the high point, or low point depending on the perspective of the characters. It was when whatever's going to happen happens, what the whole story was driving toward. I knew denouement was the resolution, the part where things get explained or made clear. Ebert never got further than writing *climax* on the board. Tommy jumped all over that, if you know what I mean.

We went back to silent reading. Except Mr. Ebert wasn't reading. He was writing fast. I wondered if it was a manifesto, the thing that shows up on the internet after he's killed a few hundred people.

The difference between climax and denouement didn't matter to me. They both answered the question: how does it end? For me, so much had ended already. I looked over at Axel. He was looking outside. The wind was whipping a confession from the maple tree. Its leaves had been red all along. I couldn't even trust the trees. The leaves weren't the only things changing. Something was coming. It wasn't just winter.

Axel was the first to leave when the bell rang. I saw him glance at Ebert's document. On the way out of class, I paused to get a glimpse. Beneath it, the newspaper was open to the classified ads. I bent to take a closer look, but Tommy took hold of my ponytail and yanked my head back.

We were all a victim of the No Child Left Behind policy. Tommy should still have been in kindergarten where pulling hair was a thing. Instead, he was there in high school tormenting me.

"The new kid is over you, huh? Let me guess. You let him bust your encryption, if you know what I mean."

I punched him right in his glassy eyeball. Only in my daydream. Revealing what I could do to Chatham had lost me Axel. I walked away. I could still hear Tommy talking in his robot voice. "Please insert disk. Please insert disk," he said. Except every time he repeated it, it sounded less like *disk* and more like [illegible].

We had assigned seats in Reynold's class, but I sat as far away from Axel as I could and stared at the surface of the desk. Why did they try to give it a wood grain? Everyone knew it was fake. Darcy's false nails came into my field of vision as she tapped on the desk. "That's not your seat."

I looked up at her without lifting my head. I didn't say a word. She found another seat.

Chatham laid a hand on my shoulder, and I clamped my hand over his and turned on him. I guess I was jumpy. I can only imagine what my expression looked like. Those blue/gold eyes of his went wide for a minute. I tried on a smile just for his benefit.

"You all right?"

Was I? I never gave him an answer. I squeezed his hand before I let him go and turned back to the front of the room. I could almost feel Darcy's eyes on me, like sharp fingernails. I didn't care. I could almost feel Axel not looking at me. That was what hurt.

Mr. Reynolds was writing *rule of law* and *due process* on the board with his left hand in his usual careful, deliberate script. He underlined the words with his red marker. He stared at them for a long time before he asked us what they meant. I knew the answer: we as a people abided by laws that were fairly drawn up and fairly enforced. I didn't say that out loud. Right then, I didn't think anything was fair.

He picked up his remote. Pictures of popular culture began to flash across the screen. He hadn't erased the board so what he'd written showed through like a bloodstain on the images of Starsky and Hutch, Dirty Harry, the team from *Lethal Weapon*, *Buffy the Vampire Slayer*, *The Batman*, every Avenger. And now, faces we didn't recognize. Protesters being tear-gassed. Police beating an unarmed man.

"Which of those images were true?" Reynolds asked as he picked up the red marker again. He was looking directly at me, glaring. "Well?"

"The last ones were real," I said in a small voice.

"Aha! I said true, not real. There's a difference. There is a truth in our culture, a dirty open secret that we approve of brutality. Think of the movies you've seen. Why are we surprised when it carries over into real life? Due process means innocent until proven guilty, not the other way around. Vigilante justice isn't justice. We can't take the law into our own hands. We just can't." He made a fist, and I heard a popping noise. He'd crushed the marker. It was staining his hand red. He didn't even notice.

After a while he went back to his desk. He didn't mention anything to us about silent reading, but I could see from where I sat, he had the newspaper spread out before him. He spent the rest of the period staring down at it.

The class felt no obligation to be silent. There was a lot of chatter about what people were wearing for the game the next day. Remember, I mentioned homecoming coincided with Halloween this year. No one was thinking about rights and due process, just tricks and treats.

They were also talking about our chances of winning the next day. No one knew if Chatham was going to be cleared through concussion protocols. If not, Kamal would be the starting quarterback in his place.

We got called down to the gym for the pep rally before class ended. As I passed Reynolds' desk, I got a closer look at what he was reading. It was the classified section. The ad for babysitting was still there. So was the one for an exterminator, but it was slightly different. Now, it said: *Last Call. DEADline approaching. Must act now to receive incentive. Dead* was capitalized and put in bold. I didn't know what the message was really saying, but it couldn't be good.

I didn't go to the rally. Pep was not something I was feeling.

Record Group No. 13

On Saturday Jenny told me my uncle was leaving ██████. I wasn't hearing voices. Not back then at least. Now in this cell, I'm not so sure. Sometimes I think I hear Axel calling my name. I don't know if it's in my mind. Maybe they're playing a recording to drive me crazy. They're not going to have to drive very far.

I was in the kitchen at my uncle's house. The homecoming game was starting at two p.m. It was about noon. I figured I was going to need fuel for whatever was coming. I still didn't exactly know what was going to happen. I had a good idea it would involve terror and mayhem. Those things don't sit well on an empty stomach.

The cupboards were completely empty. So was the refrigerator. My uncle had never kept the place stocked, but I'd never seen it this bare. Then I saw the Jennys in a duffle bag on the kitchen table. It was open and I caught a glimpse of the block of eight stamps on top. My uncle's retirement plan. He'd taken them out of the glass case in the basement. He was in a rush. Otherwise, he would have wrapped them in something, wouldn't he have?

He was leaving. I was sure he wouldn't take me with him. He also wouldn't leave me here in one piece. My first thought was to run away. I went to the kitchen door. It wouldn't budge. I glanced into the hallway and heard my uncle coming up the stairs from the basement. He was between me and the front door.

Axel had given me a cell phone early on. I'll admit now I carried it with me wherever I went. I'd even slept with it on the off-chance Axel might have needed me for anything at all at any time. I dialed his number. He didn't answer. There was no way to leave a message. I took a pot from a cabinet, filled it with water and put it on the stove to boil. It gave me something to do. I'd heard the phrase: a watched pot never boils, so I observed my uncle instead, hoping he'd go down into the basement just one more time. He didn't.

He came into the kitchen, filling the doorframe. He stretched out his fingers, cracking his knuckles. I wondered if that's what it would sound like when he broke every bone in my body.

He took a step toward me.

"Were you my mother's brother or my father's?"

He paused like he had to think about it. "Let's just say I am a friend of the extended family."

"On my mother's side?"

"I am getting tired of your questions," he said.

"I think I've asked you like five since I've lived with you."

"I'm even more tired of your attitude."

He took two slow steps toward me and backhanded me across the face so hard I saw Pluto and some other stars. I stumbled back against the stove and felt a few drops of scalding liquid spray out of the pot onto my back.

Sparring with Axel, I would have responded with a punch, and a kick, and a knee to the groin, not necessarily in that order. This was different; this was family.

I put a hand to my cheek and stared up at my uncle. He looked radiant.

He sighed. "I've been wanting to do that for a very long time."

There was a light in his eyes. He was making the same mistake every bad guy made in every bad movie. He was going to mix business and pleasure. He probably had orders to kill me; he most definitely wanted to enjoy it.

He struck me on the other cheek. I let it spin me around, so I was facing the stove. He grabbed hold of my ponytail. I didn't fight back. What could I do to him? He was a thick wall of flesh and bone. He probably didn't even feel pain. I remember Axel telling me, "Use what you've got." I made up a rule of my own. Use what they have against them. What they love.

I picked up the pot of water. It wasn't boiling yet, but any liquid would do the trick. I flung its contents toward the table, and the open bag. I'm sorry, Jenny. The boiling water hit the block of stamps. It was like licking them all at once with a giant hot tongue. They changed shape as they glued themselves to whatever lay beneath them. They went from pristine to used in a split second. From priceless to worthless.

My uncle screamed. More importantly, he let me go. The pot, now empty, never stopped moving. I raised it in an arc and brought it back around and caught him in the temple. He barely blinked, but he slipped on the slick wet linoleum, and gravity and his own momentum brought him down. The back of his head clipped the corner of the Formica table. I didn't stop to see if he was okay, or better yet, dead. I ran.

I didn't look back as my pounding steps crunched the falling leaves, even though I would never come this way again. I should have been overjoyed. I had been right about my fake uncle. I had bested him. There was no time for celebration.

He was the first casualty on a list that by the end of the day would be as long as my arm.

Record Group No. 14

I made it to the school without stopping. I was barely out of breath when I got there. I was working off a powerful cocktail of conditioning and adrenalin.

A homecoming game has its own soundtrack. Marching band music is like elevator music. You take something catchy and take the words out and everything else that is good about it. The only difference is elevator music doesn't make you want to jump on someone and knock them to the ground. The stadium was filling, the scent of hot dogs floated on the crisp autumn air. Even without the music, I sensed a thrum of energy and excitement.

I had the phone that Axel had given me. I hit the send button over and over. Axel didn't pick up. He would know what I should do. I felt I couldn't call the police. What could they do? I'd end up in foster care, where my uncle—if he was still alive—could find me. Or his people would.

For a while, I played a version of "Where's Waldo" in the crowd. I actually found him. Remember, it was Halloween? Think of every costume you've ever seen and put it in that stadium. The majority of spectators, however, had chosen the lazy man's costume: zombies. Ripped jeans were already fashionable, so all they had to do was put black circles under their eyes, gray powder in their hair and sketch out some fake blood here and there with a tube of lipstick.

By the end of the day, it wouldn't all be fake.

I let myself into the high school and peered through the glass panes in every door. Everything was normal. I went down into the tunnel that connects to the football stadium. There were some football players milling around. I thought it odd this close to gametime they weren't in the locker room for the pep talk before I realized those were kids in costumes. I tested the door to the AV room. It was locked as usual.

Chatham came out of the locker room and leaned a shoulder against the wall next to me.

We looked at each other. He was dressed like a grown-up in a suit and tie, but it wasn't a costume. It meant he was still benched because of his concussion and couldn't wear his uniform. I had a vision of him coming home from a day at the office. All he was missing was a briefcase full of cares and a crease in his smooth forehead.

"How are you feeling?" I asked.

"Better. The doctor said I can play again."

"How come you're not suited up?"

"I didn't want to ruin it for Kamal. If I'm out, he's the starting quarterback."

He leaned in close enough so that I could see the pupils in his blue-gold eyes. They were sleek ravens in a wheat field against a clear blue sky. He wore cologne. It was strong and smelled like mountain streams, fireplace smoke, and regular mortgage payments. He lowered his voice. "Don't tell anyone. It's supposed to be a surprise. Kamal's dad came all the way from █████ to see this."

"Kamal's father? Is here? Is out there? In the stadium?"

He nodded.

I cursed, but it doesn't matter here what I said. I pulled out my phone from the pocket of my hoodie. I tried Axel again.

"What's the matter?" Chatham asked.

"Kamal's not the target."

"Target? What are you talking about?"

The ground underneath me shook as the marching band hit a high note. I didn't have time to fill Chatham in. I tried Axel again. Finally, he answered. Chatham and I made a huddle around the phone, facing the concrete wall, trying to block out the noise in the hallway. If I hadn't turned my back on the devils and zombies behind me, everything might have turned out differently. Out of the corner of my eye I remember seeing a killer clown, a president, and a puffed-up dinosaur. I should have paid closer attention.

"Now is not a good time, Talya." It sounded like Axel was talking through gritted teeth.

"Kamal's father is here," I said. "In the stands."

He cursed like he meant it. "Why the hell wasn't I informed?" he muttered to himself. "This is the perfect place and time for an assassination. There's no security here. They can just pick him off in the crowd with all the chaos."

"What chaos?"

He didn't answer my question. "You've got to get to him first," he said instead.

"Me?" He'd told me I was no longer involved. "What about you?"

"I've got my hands full at the moment," he said meaningfully. "Of wires."

Was he talking about a bomb? I should have asked him where he was. I should have asked him exactly what he meant by "get to him first." All I could do was stare at Chatham as he stared back at me.

"Shhhhhh," Axel whispered harshly. He didn't need to say it, I was already speechless.

Around me another tremor made the concrete shake as the drums above us beat in unison. I covered the mic with my thumb and stared up at Chatham. We waited for Axel to talk. The building shook again in tune with the marching band. I could feel the crowd stamping against the floor of the stands.

Above us there was the clashing of cymbals. On the other end of the line came the ugly tearing boom of a gunshot. It was so loud, so present, it felt like I'd been hit. I shuddered. I dropped the phone. By the time I picked it up with shaking hands, Axel was gone.

"What was that?" Chatham asked as his eyes went wide.

I didn't answer. Axel. Gone. My brain threatened to go offline. I redirected my focus to the mission Axel had given me. Get to Kamal's father first.

I barged into the football locker room, vaguely aware that Chatham followed me in.

"It's kill or be…" Coach Schuhmann stopped in the middle of his pep talk. I doubt he knew he wasn't talking figuratively.

"Kamal, get your father on the phone," I said.

It must have been a rousing speech I interrupted. Coach's face was already red. It turned a deeper shade of scarlet. "What the hell is she doing in here?"

I ignored him. "Call your father, now!" I said to Kamal. "Tell him to get down. Under the seats. Tell him not to run, or they'll pick him off."

I realize now, of course, that oversharing is never a good thing. I should have saved that last piece of information until the line was established. Kamal dropped the phone. I knew enough not to tell him to hurry. Making an already nervous person more nervous doesn't help anybody. My blood was pumping hard. My focus was narrowing. But Coach Schuhmann was big enough to fit into anyone's peripheral vision.

"Chatham, get her out of here," he said.

"Just listen to her," he said.

"If you won't, then I will."

"I wouldn't do that," Chatham was saying. But Coach did. I blocked his sweaty ham hand. He tried again. I blocked that too. I wondered if this was what it was like to work in a butcher shop. I didn't have time for a part-time job. I took a step away from him. Maybe he thought I was leaving. Instead, I jump-kicked him back against the lockers, and he landed in a heap on the concrete floor.

I had the team's attention. Kamal pounded a fist against his phone. "My father's not answering. He must not be able to hear it."

We all looked up as the room vibrated. If only I could silence the damned marching band. I had a brief fantasy of putting a bullet straight through the brass section. I'd never be able to shoot fast enough to take them all out at once.

"Try again," I said. We all waited to that vibrating soundtrack. It was a song we once knew that had been beaten unrecognizable by the percussion section.

Kamal looked up at me with pleading eyes. "What are we going to do?"

"Get to him first," I said. "Where's he sitting?"

"Bleacher section, thirty-yard line."

"That's right across from the press box," I said.

"They'll see you coming," Chatham said in a low voice. "They'll shoot him before you can get to him."

"Not if I shoot him first."

I shouldn't have said it out loud. Or so that Kamal could hear me. But I didn't have time to massage the truth.

"I'll wing him," I said to console Kamal. It didn't seem to work. He let out what I can only describe as a wail.

"He'll go down and be surrounded by people. Whoever is after him will show themselves. They'll be the only ones looking my way." I said it like I had planned it out, not like it came to me as I was speaking.

"You all stay here," I said, but Kamal came at me. I think he was heading for the exit, to go to his father. In any case, Chatham blocked him and held him by the shoulders.

"Stay here," I said to the rest of the team. I didn't threaten them. I had nothing to threaten them with. I've had time to think about it now. It's like teaching. Either you command respect, or you don't. The fact that I had commanded Coach Schuhmann to the other side of the locker room probably hadn't hurt.

I went down the hallway. I didn't bother to pick the lock to the range. I kicked the knob so hard it came off, and the door swung open. I did the same to the bank of lockers. The padlocks were new; the latches were fifty years old. I pulled out my rifle first, then opened the ammunition case by slamming the butt of my rifle into the glass door. I filled the pockets of my hoodie with bullets, then I picked up as many rifles as I could carry and went back to the locker room. The players were all standing where I'd left them. I think they may have been in shock.

Chatham had to hold Kamal even harder when he saw the rifles. I dropped them onto the closest bench, picked one up, loaded it, and went to Chatham.

"I don't know what's going to happen. Don't let anyone in here. Or out of here."

Kamal started to struggle against Chatham's iron grip. Hindsight is 20/20. In retrospect I should not have approached him with a loaded .22 in my hands.

I tried to soften my tone. "You've got to stay here, Kamal. It's for your own safety. In the meantime, keep trying to get your father on the phone. This is only a last resort. Do you have a picture of him?"

"I won't show you."

I'd been training my reflexes. I had his phone and was scrolling one-handed to the camera before he could even protest. His dad looked just like him, but with a mustache. I handed the phone back.

I gave the loaded rifle to Chatham. "Kamal does not leave this room. If he tries, shoot him."

There was that keening wail again. "Not in a vital organ," I added too late.

The side of beef on the floor by the lockers let out a grunt. "Same goes for Coach." I pulled a handful of bullets from my pocket and tossed them onto the bench with the rifles, like it was trick or treat. I loaded my own rifle and turned to find Chatham standing in front of me.

"You can't do this."

"Please, Chatham, I don't want to hurt you." I had armed him, but I was confident I could outshoot him.

"You can't do it alone."

"I'll take the hallway through here to the press box, shoot from there."

"The school's security officer hangs out up there. You need someone watching the crowd. You need blockers."

I wasn't fluent in the language of football, but I could imagine what a blocker was. I was running out of time. I'd like to say I talked Chatham into it. It would probably help his case. But I can't lie. I don't believe the truth will set me free. Or Chatham. He's looking at twenty years, isn't he? There are some things I did on that day that I don't regret at all. They needed to be done. Getting Chatham involved? I feel bad about that.

When I didn't say anything, he picked up some bullets and stuffed them into the pocket of his dress pants.

He turned back to Kamal. "Trust me, brother."

"I do," Kamal said through clenched teeth as he motioned to me. "But do you trust this…"

I knew he wanted to say *girl.* Maybe even *little girl.* His eyes flicked to Coach who was still lying like a heap of sweaty laundry on the locker room floor.

"I do trust her," Chatham said. "I trust her with my life."

Dear God, I thought, *please don't let it come to that.*

Chatham clapped Kamal on the shoulder, then looked at the boys around him.

"Atkins, Carson, Henderson, you're with us," he said, handing rifles all around. I knew them only well enough to know what sounded like last names were their first. Later, I would feel bad about involving them too. At that moment, all I regretted was that those painted-on football tights didn't have pockets to hold bullets.

Record Group No. 15

We headed out through the back of the locker room into the hallway that led to the press box. I was in the middle with Chatham and his group flanking me. The hallway was empty. We didn't need to hide our guns, which was good, because there aren't many places to put a long rifle. We ran to what would have been midfield, up the stairs, burst through the door to the press box and the boys had the room cleared out in less than five seconds. No one in the crowd noticed. All eyes were on the midfield, on the midriffs of the cheerleaders who were working themselves into a frenzy of pompoms to the throbbing of the marching band. I took everything in. The long table with microphones and, just beyond it, the short wall and the wide-open view out onto the field and across to the other side of the stadium.

I zeroed in on Kamal's father with just my eyes for now. I might accidentally kill him, and I didn't even know his name. It was better not to think about that and just do the math. A football field is fifty-three yards across. He was in the third row from the sidelines. The press box was probably five yards back, twenty rows up. That bullet was going to lose three to four inches in height during its trajectory. The air was cold and clear. No wind.

I half-jumped, half-slid over the table and sank down with my back against the short wall. Chatham took a knee in front of me. He had shed his suit jacket somewhere in the tunnel and had yanked his tie down. He looked a little like Superman.

I closed my eyes. You might think I went far away from the stadium, away from the thumping of the marching band, the shrill cries of the cheerleaders, and the murmur of the crowd. I didn't. I went to the basement of the school. Axel was there.

"I believe in you, Talya. You can do this."

My eyes flew open. "Shut up, Chatham, just please shut up! I know I can do it. I've got to get my heart rate down. I've got to get to a place of peace."

I closed my eyes again. Axel cupped my chin in his warm hand and looked deep into my eyes. I put my hands on either side of his face. I could feel the roughness of his stubble as I pulled him close and kissed him once hard on the mouth.

"I believe in you, Talya. You can do this." It was the same thing Chatham had said to me. Don't judge. I was about to let off a shot in a stadium full of innocent bystanders at a distance of at least sixty yards, which was at the upper end of that rifle's capacity. I didn't have time to be creative.

Axel disappeared and I saw my reflection in the mirror of my mind's eye. She looked grim and determined. And impatient. "Do this!" she echoed.

I opened my eyes, pushed my glasses up, turned, and placed my .22 on top of the short wall, swinging it twenty degrees to my left until my target (it was better not to think of him as human) was in my sights. I didn't forget my calculations, but I didn't let them rule me. I let instinct and experience take over. I zeroed in on his shoulder, took one last breath, held it and squeezed the trigger in a gentle fluid motion.

I always forget how loud the retort of a rifle is. It was close, it was real, and what the hell had I just done? Kamal's father went down. The shot didn't blow him directly backward. He spun sharply before falling. That made me ~~think~~ ~~hope~~ pray I had only winged him. It took a moment for the chain reaction I had started to spread.

Some of the spectators turned to where my shot had landed, some leaned over Kamal's father. Some started to run the other way. It's hard to run in the bleachers. I'd been practicing. They toppled. And the band played on. The cheerleaders cheered. I was already reloading. Closer to us, spectators ducked their heads at the shot or turned toward us and saw the rifle. For a moment there was shock and stillness, then the crowd started to fan out like a house of cards collapsing. Or I wished it had been like that. Cards would have been easier to step over.

Chatham pointed to the sidelines below us. "The president," he yelled.

I had to stand to look over the wall. Of course, it wasn't our real president, it was someone in a suit and a rubber mask, standing behind the state-of-the-art telescopic camera that was mounted on a tripod. I wonder if that's why I hesitated. I'd just shot an innocent man, but there's something so ingrained about the importance of that presidential office, that even a fake president commands some respect deep down in our psyche.

His eye holes were pointed straight at me. Sometimes a telephoto lens is just a telephoto lens. When he swiveled it in my direction, I realized he wasn't going to just shoot a picture. I ducked as the digital clock exploded above my head. You can't kill time, but it seemed to slow after that.

I brought my head up even as shards of glass and metal were floating down like confetti. The president and I fired at the same time. He hit the bullhorn mounted to the press box. I missed. I'd never fired while under fire. It's not easy. I dropped behind the press box wall, reloaded, and raised my head again. I should have realized he had a better weapon. He could have and would have blown my head off, but he was running now.

Chatham and his crew were already going over the wall, and I followed. I landed on something, maybe someone. I didn't stop to check. The bleachers were emptying but not fast enough. Chatham cleared the way as best he could. By that, I mean he threw people out of the way. Still, it was slow going. The field was starting to fill, the "president" ahead of the pack with a clear goal—the end zone and the tunnel just beyond it that ended in the school basement.

He had left his rifle on the tripod, but I assumed he was armed with something smaller. He was closing the distance to the gaggle of cheerleaders. The color guard had let their flags fall. They stood looking around, not sure what to do. It wouldn't be much longer until I lost my chance for a good shot. I paused and let the boys go ahead, waited until I had a clear bead and fired.

I blew his leg out from under him, and he went down hard. I still couldn't see his face, but as I reloaded, I realized who he was. Maybe I had known subconsciously all along. I've had plenty of time to think about why I hadn't aimed for his right leg—his good leg.

Reynolds reached out and grabbed a mock rifle from the color sergeant, using it as a crutch to pull himself up and continue on. He wasn't record-setting fast, but he had an advantage—the chaos between him and us.

The crowd in the bleachers was aware of us now and was moving out of our way. We pounded down those metal benches in sync. One after the other we hit the field. I had my eyes on Reynolds, trying to catch one last glimpse of him before I lost the high ground. I lost my footing and rolled, but I was up in a fluid motion.

We scattered the cheerleaders in a flurry of pompoms. I saw Chatham literally knock Darcy out of the way. It brought me no joy, not one single iota. I thought: *he's a dead man.* I prayed that wasn't foreshadowing.

We moved forward as one, with Chatham leading the way. Was it years of practice in running plays, or something he was born with? It didn't matter. He had an awareness of his own physicality and that of those around him, and a command of the field that adapted to every unpredictable change ahead of us. The pounding of the marching band devolved into a cacophony of horns until they finally fell silent. My heartbeat swelled to replace its rhythm. It was strong and steady, as deliberate as a drum.

In that moment, I understood the fascination with war and other team sports. To be part of a group against an overwhelming majority. Us against all the rest of them with nothing but determination, motivation, the butt of our rifles, and the unwavering belief we were in the right. In the light of reason (or an interrogation lamp) did we do some things that were wrong? Sometimes you have to do wrong to do right.

Chatham was a boy, really. Eighteen on the verge of nineteen, but I saw him as a leader of men in his future. Does he still have a future?

I can't bear to think about the future now, and I wasn't thinking about it then. Everything was now. We pounded forward, every step in sync with our hearts. Every heart in sync with the other. There were five of us moving forward as one vanguard. It's said you can't get anywhere without stepping on someone. People went down. I wasn't counting how many. I only noticed they were in my way.

The field was starting to clear, and the stragglers? Let's just say it's easier to mow down someone if they're headed in the same direction you're going. Reynolds fired a shot. I want to think it was into the air. I don't know if he hurt anyone. Directly at least. But indirectly, what happened next was really his fault, not mine. A whole zombie apocalypse turned toward us as one. They were trying to get away from that shot, but that meant they'd have to go through us.

They were desperate. So was I. The difference between us was I'd been training for this for the last sixty-one days. Oh, and I had a weapon.

Chatham was calling plays I didn't understand. I couldn't speak his language. I let the butt of my rifle do the talking. The responses were universal: grunts, groans, cracks, and screams as we clashed together with the crowd. I used my shoulders, my feet, my hands. I never once used nice words.

The waves kept coming. We kept going over them. Atkins got swept away, then Carson and finally Henderson. Chatham and I went on, shoulder to shoulder. When the zombie apocalypse finally folded, we saw what we were really up against. A row of four ~~security guards~~ armed security guards.

I didn't hesitate. I kicked one and at the same time hit the other in the head with the butt of my rifle. They never touched me, but the pure physics of that move brought me to the ground. The third guard saw an opportunity to pounce on me. From the corner of my eye, I saw Chatham swing the fourth into the sidelines, then he was tearing number three off of me and tossing him away.

He gave me his hand and I scrambled up. Behind him I saw security guards three and four getting up and coming at us.

"Chatham!" I said to warn him. He gave my hand a squeeze, blinked at me with both eyes, and pushed me toward the end zone. He turned away. I did too. I heard the impact behind me, the grunts and the struggle. I moved on. I had to. Later I was glad I'd held his hand that one last time. It was as close as I'd ever get to saying goodbye. I was alone again. I'd been used to that these last years. Now it felt wrong.

Reynolds had been right. His disability had made him invisible. The guards had let him slip by without a glance. I sprinted into the end zone, sending Little Red Riding Hood and a wolf careening into the padding on the goal posts. I didn't even look both ways, as I skidded into the tunnel. I turned right. I can't say I saw Reynolds go that way, or that I heard him. I sensed him.

I shoved a killer clown out of my way who hit the wall so hard he bounced back into my path. I felt like I was playing one of those games at the county fair when I knocked him out of my way again. I didn't know my own strength. This wasn't a matter of degree. It was full-fledged, all-out war against one man. I had to stop Reynolds. I had to get to Axel.

When the clown went down and stayed down, I could see Tommy standing against the wall with another stoner. Rings of smoke circled their heads.

"Get down!" I yelled. No one ever listens in a situation like that. People don't do as they're told, they just turn and stare at you. I moved a couple bystanders out of the way, again with the butt of my rifle, again for their own good. "Get down!" I yelled again. All I did was waste my breath and let Reynolds know exactly where I was. He turned, lost his balance and was falling, but let off a shot that would have blown my head off, if I hadn't hit the ground. The bullet ricocheted off the concrete wall somewhere behind me. I heard a yelp as someone got hit. I figured if they could make a sound, they were probably alive. I never looked around to check. Reynolds had landed on his back and was twisting around to get at me again.

I was bringing my rifle around. I didn't bother getting up. Prone position is how I'd learned to shoot on the rifle team. Having my elbow against the cold concrete gave me the stability I needed. This time I didn't hesitate. I should have aimed for his core. I still don't know why I didn't. Maybe it made sense to me to take out the gun. Maybe I was confident I'd hit him where it counted at close range. I still didn't know where Axel was, and I was pretty sure he did. Maybe I just couldn't bring myself to kill my favorite teacher.

~~Things happen~~. You make things happen that you can't undo. If you live, you have all the time in the world to second guess yourself. I fired and blew the gun out of his good hand. Along with some of his fingers. When you shoot someone, it only takes an instant. I've had plenty of time to think about that, and it still makes me sick. I didn't have the luxury of empathizing right then.

I grabbed the 9mm from where it had slid into the wall. It was slick and I didn't want to think about why. I dropped down beside Reynolds, holding his gun. I cringed at the expression of pain on his face. What scared me more was the determination I saw there.

"Where is Axel?"

Reynolds didn't say a word.

Tommy knelt next to him. The haze of smoke around him was gone, along with the glassy expression. "Here, let me try." He made a fist and raised it up. I blocked it.

"No! I believe in due process." I believed everything Reynolds had taught us. Torture wasn't the best way to get information out of someone. I believed him when he'd said it in class. What I believed more was the hard line of his lips. "Please, Mr. Reynolds. You're not a bad man." I felt that deep down, despite the fact he had fired on me.

Just then one of the players opened the locker room door and peeked out. Reynold's face hardened, as if he remembered what his mission was. "What the hell are you doing? I told you to stay put," I yelled.

"I heard shots," the player said.

"Which is more reason to stay inside. Shut the door." I pointed the 9mm at him. He stood there stunned. I aimed just left of him and fired into the concrete. The shockwave of the shot was amplified by the concrete all around us. It made me deaf for a second, so I didn't actually hear him scream.

Technically, I didn't hit him. Technically, it was the ricocheting bullet or a piece of concrete. I could see even from a distance, it was a flesh wound. He looked down at his bicep and saw the red. His eyes rolled back in his head, and he fell backward as the door fell shut behind him.

I had lost my small window of opportunity.

"Please, Mr. Reynolds," I said. It struck me later that even after all he'd done, I couldn't drop the mister. "I'm begging you. Please. Tell me. Axel's all I have."

It was the wrong thing to say. "My wife was all I had," he said violently. "They promised her… I promised her safety. She risked her life for me, and they sent her back."

My vision wasn't so clear anymore. I was seeing the world through a thin layer of water. I was drowning. Still, out of the corner of my eye I could see Tommy raise his fist again. I yanked him back by the collar.

"You're not a bad man," I said again to Mr. Reynolds. "You were…you are a good teacher. I believe what you taught me."

It's what every teacher wants to hear. It's deeper than flattery or bribery. Deep down we all need a purpose. We all need to know this isn't for nothing.

"You were…" I tried to erase the past tense. "You're my favorite teacher." I didn't say anything more. I waited, one hand still on the 9mm, not exactly pointing it at him. The other was on Tommy's collar pinning his face against the concrete floor.

Reynolds didn't say a word, but he seemed to really see me. He winced. His eyes flicked left to the AV room.

Record Group No. 16

I knew Reynolds kept his keys on a lanyard. I pulled them off his belt. I was at the door in just a few steps. I'd been so close all this time, standing outside there with Chatham. The realization that I was right here and still might be too late, made me even later. My hands were shaking. I dropped the keys, then couldn't find the right one.

I vaguely registered Tommy knocking Reynolds out, but I had other issues. I stepped away from the door and fired Reynold's 9mm. I went deaf again for a few moments and couldn't hear Tommy cursing next to me. I only saw his mouth moving. I entered the AV room. I sensed him follow me, but all I saw was Axel. And the pool of blood. He'd lost so much, I could have done a back stroke in it.

He was lying parallel to the sound board. The panel was off. He still held a long wire clutched in his hand. I knelt on his right side, where I could see Reynolds' feet through the open door. Tommy knelt down next to me. He was taking off his T-shirt and pressing it against the hole in Axel's upper chest and shoulder. It was the same Pink Floyd shirt he'd worn when Axel had banged his head against the desk. I saw that Tommy was way too ripped for a stoner.

"Put pressure on the wound," Tommy said. I was already doing it. The only other people I'd loved in this world had bled to death. I wasn't going to let it happen again. I'd read up on trauma. I knew what I had to do. That doesn't mean you can ever be prepared for what it feels like.

Tommy had pulled a cell phone from his back pocket and was speaking into it in a language I couldn't understand. He said something about a code ten and about a suspect having been subdued and asked whoever he was talking to to respond to the southern entrance of the stadium. He laid his phone down by Axel's head and seemed to notice the open panel for the first time. He cursed again, except it sounded like he was praying. "Is that a bomb?"

Can you believe I had forgotten about it? "Um, yeah, I guess," I said. I felt sick. All that blood, Axel's, Reynolds', Kamal's father's, which I couldn't see but still felt on my hands. And now the realization that I'd insisted Kamal stay in the locker room. Right down the hall from a bomb.

Tommy was grabbing my arm as if he wanted to get up and drag me out with him. "Axel defused it," I said, even though I had no idea if that was true. I must have said it with enough conviction because Tommy sank back down. He put two fingers to Axel's throat feeling for a pulse.

"What the hell is going on?" Tommy asked me. I didn't know where to start. It had all gotten so complicated. I thought back to the beginning, had a flashback of Axel walking into Ebert's English class. Of him sitting behind me. The way he noticed me that first day.

Axel opened his eyes and looked right at me. I could tell he wasn't seeing me. He was there, but not there. Those penetrating, brown, beautiful eyes were empty windows. His breath was coming in shallow gasps. His eyes rolled back into his head. In the movies, this is the romantic part where I'd beg him to stay with me. I'd tell him over and over it was going to be okay. In reality, I clamped down even harder onto his shoulder bone and a soft groan escaped his lips. But then he went limp.

Tommy was still checking for a pulse. He shook his head ever so slightly.

"No! It has to be there. Let me try." I took my hands from Axel's shoulder, from inside his shoulder, and Tommy replaced them. I put my fingers to Axel's throat. I felt no throb of life there. Maybe I just didn't know exactly where to look.

"You can't do this," I said. I realize dying is something that happens to you, but in that moment, I blamed Axel. I've had plenty of time to think about what I did next. You might assume I had seen this in a movie once, but that wasn't how it was.

My heart was shattering into a million crystalline pieces. I wanted to break his. I wanted him to know exactly what I felt, except the dead—those lucky bastards—can't feel anything.

You've heard of those mothers who for a split second have the superhuman strength to lift a car off their babies? I had that strength. I could feel it gathering like a storm inside me. Instead of concentrating it upwards, I clasped my hands together, raised them up and brought them down on Axel's chest with all my strength, rage, love, and desperation.

I didn't break his heart. What I heard was the cracking of his ribs. But I must have wounded it at least because a trickle of blood flowed out the side of his mouth. His body trembled. He made a sound that was a gasp and a gurgle in one.

Beside me Tommy prayed/cursed again. "You really are a [illegible] machine."

Suddenly he raised his hands into the air. Automatically, I put mine back into Axel's shoulder before I looked up. First, I registered the guns. There were three of them. Behind them, with angry faces, were three of the four security guards Chatham and I had "blocked" on the field. They told me to put my hands up. Believe it or not, I was surprised. I thought by now, after they saw Reynolds, that they'd realize I was the good guy in this story. It dawned on me that's not how it might look to everyone else. I had shot Kamal's father, an unarmed man. For good reason, but context is everything and they didn't have the backstory.

They asked me to put my [illegible] hands up. I shook my head.

"I can't. He'll bleed out. I'm not leaving him until you get someone in here to help him."

They looked at each other and their guns waved back and forth. As badly as they wanted to subdue me, they wanted even less to be where I was and get their hands dirty. One of them plucked a radio from his belt and spoke in that shorthand language Tommy had used, then sent one of his partners outside to wait for the ambulance. That left two of them. My arms were aching, even though I had them locked at the elbow, my weight above them for leverage. I shifted, and their arms straightened as their hands got twitchy. I wasn't scared. I felt a calm spread over me, as if the warmth of Axel's blood was flowing up to my heart and all through my extremities. Love makes a lousy bullet-proof vest, but at that moment I felt invincible. I didn't think I couldn't die; I was willing to die for him.

I looked down at Axel. As with the only other people in my life I'd really loved, I had no picture of him. I studied him. I knew I was cramming for a test I'd eventually fail. The years make mental photographs fade. I tried so hard to hang onto him, the long lashes, the insistent stubble on his chin. If only I could see his dark brown eyes again. If only I could see that sardonic half smile again. A black boot threatened to photobomb my mental picture. I looked up and the security guard stopped inching forward. I would have laughed if I could have. What did he think I was going to do, knuckle-deep in Axel's shoulder? Shoot him with my eyes?

I saw two light blue uniforms appear by the door with a stretcher. Why weren't they coming in?

"I won't let him go until you get your hands on him. Please. I won't hurt you."

One of the security guards laughed, a short bark that broke the tension. They realized I was just what I looked like, a broken-hearted girl covered with tears and blood. I looked down at Axel like it was the last time. Even if he lived, I might never see him again. *If.* Such a small word. Such a powerful word. There was so much to say. I didn't get the chance. He wouldn't have heard me if I had.

It's hard to remember exactly what happened next. My hands were being pushed aside. A mask was going over Axel's face. That beautiful face. Then Tommy pulled something out of his back pocket and all the guns swiveled in his direction. "I'm on the job," he said.

Job? Tommy? I thought about what I'd said to Axel: that Tommy had to reach for the stars because no one on earth would hire him. I thought about how it made Axel laugh, how his dark eyes had lit up.

Tommy fumbled and dropped something in Axel's blood. It was a small wallet. I was having trouble focusing, but I saw Tommy's picture, and a name that wasn't his. It was a badge.

I barely noticed the guns swivel back in my direction.

"You?" I said. "But—" Maybe I was part robot because I short-circuited. My mind snapped shut as if the power had been turned off. A nanosecond later, my thoughts sizzled back online. I blinked. My vision narrowed. The guards around me were inching closer, but I only registered their uniforms in a vague blue and black haze. "You bullied me," I said to Tommy.

"You noticed everything. I had to protect my cover."

"But—" There was that split second of lag again as my brain glitched. What he said next made it all click into place with a clarity that gave me almost an electric jolt.

"It was nothing personal."

The barrel of a gun crossed into my field of vision. It's not that I ignored it. All I could see was Tommy shrugging as he gave me a sheepish smile.

"It *was* personal. It *is* personal."

I wiped that smile off his face. With my fist. Over and over. I didn't care about the guns. Once or twice, I must have missed, because, later, I realized my knuckles were broken. It was like an out of body experience. I take complete responsibility for everything I did that day up to that point. After that, I was no longer in control. I was on autopilot. As much as I hate to admit it, Tommy had been right about me. I *was* a robot. In the distance I heard words repeating like on a recorded loop: "does that compute?" It took me awhile to realize it was me.

The homecoming game never took place, but I know what it's like to be tackled and buried under a pile of knees and elbows. Afterward when I could do the math, I realized it took all of the officers to subdue me. Two of them wrenched my arms back. My feet were still free, and I lashed out at Tommy and kicked him in the head. He lost consciousness and I stopped kicking. I no longer had anything to fight against.

I sagged, and they let me fall. I counted five guns trained on me. They didn't have to worry. It was over. I was over. I saw everything as if from a distance. Tommy's still form, the guns, the wires, the bomb. Axel's blood.

He was gone. They'd taken him, and I never got to say goodbye because I'd been too busy turning Tommy's face to mush.

A security guard came into my field of vision. He may have been the one that had met the butt of my rifle on the field. He was hard to recognize. Blood was dripping from his nose onto his deep frown. My mind was still short-circuiting. Reality came back to me with the blow to the stomach he gave me. He yanked me to my feet so hard I heard a pop as he dislocated my shoulder. Pain started to kick in.

I had told Mr. Reynolds I believed in due process. I did. But did everyone else? I began to wonder if, as a prisoner, I'd be afforded the rights due me. The guard "accidentally" knocked me into the door jamb on the way out of the AV room. As my head started to bleed, I stopped wondering.

I can imagine it was hard to remove me from the AV room. My legs had turned to lead, making me a dead weight. That might be partly to blame for the way the security guard managed to hit every sharp corner on our way out of the tunnel. In a tunnel, those are hard to find. By the time we made it out into the light of day, I was bleeding from both sides of my head. The last half hour (had it even been that long?) had played out in high definition, sharper than the point of a knife. Now life seemed to have a filter in front of it. I was still aware of everything, but no longer a part of it, even though I had set it all into motion, hadn't I? My hoodie was of medium thickness, and would have been enough in the bright cold, if it hadn't been soaked. I didn't want to think about with what.

I noticed the black SUVs pull up. I didn't really register their importance until the doors opened and the black suits spilled out like ants. Except ants are small and you can step on them. These guys did the stepping. It was just like in the movies, except in real life their shoulders were a lot broader.

There was something almost non-human about them; they were walking monoliths. They didn't need to speak to make their authority obvious. One of them took the place of the guard beside me. I was in their custody now.

I spotted three ambulances in a huddle. Black suits were climbing into the driver's seats of two of them.

I couldn't tell which of the stretchers held Axel, but I screamed his name. I couldn't go to him with a tight band of steel around my upper arm. I realized later that was a hand. My head was pushed down (gently compared to the way I'd been dragged from the tunnel) as I was folded into the dark interior of the SUV. A suit climbed in next to me and we drove away with no fanfare. There was an army of sirens coming at us. Police, more ambulances, TV crews. I had never wanted attention, but the spotlight would have been safer than the dark anonymity of the SUV. I'd been afraid many times that day. About what would happen to Axel. If I'd killed Kamal's father. Now I knew a different kind of fear.

I started to shake.

Suit two leaned forward. "Hey, stop in that parking lot on the right. She might be going into shock." There wasn't a hint of alarm in his voice. He could have been requesting a trip to the drive-through at the convenience store for a cup of coffee. The driver, suit one, was handing a black case back to him from which he took a syringe. He injected it expertly into my thigh. I inhaled like a vacuum cleaner on steroids. Were those steroids? Or adrenaline. I'd been on an adrenaline-fueled kick, but it's different when it's your own. My heart did a series of somersaults before it landed where my stomach should have been. My stomach had been catapulted into my throat and was about to leave my mouth.

I groaned.

"Unlock the door," he said. I couldn't with my hands cable-tied behind my back, but I realized he wasn't talking to me. I heard the click, as he reached past me, opened the door then grabbed my hair and held my head over the pavement as my stomach, or rather its contents, flew out onto the pavement.

"Done?" he asked nonchalantly before pulling me back in. I got a glimpse of the strip mall on the outskirts of [illegible] before the door closed. It seemed so untouched. So normal compared to the scene a couple miles back.

The suit pulled a blanket from the back seat, covered me with it and tucked it in as if he was protecting cargo from being banged around until he could deliver it. There were dark stains on it. I could only imagine what they were. I didn't have to look at them long before I vomited on them. The car stopped again. The suit put on a pair of blue disposable gloves, opened the door, picked up the blanket and threw it to the side of the road. He unpeeled the gloves and threw them out after. They landed at the foot of a no-littering sign. This was an organization tasked with enforcing laws, not following them. The realization hit me harder than the irony. I didn't throw up. There was nothing left to give.

I tried to remember the route we took, to keep track of the time that passed, but my thoughts were disjointed. Other people's lives were flashing before my eyes. I saw the thin trickle of blood flowing from the corner of Axel's lip. I saw Kamal's father, flying backward. I saw Mr. Reynolds' fingers, or the lack of them. I saw Tommy's face.

The windows turn black as we drive into an underground garage. The door clanks shut behind us. The suits unload me and bring me to a room where they pass me off to a guy in a uniform, who signs for me like so much baggage.

I focus on the badge which says *security*. "Ironic, isn't it? That a secret agency uses labels," I say. He doesn't crack a smile, but my dislocated shoulder makes a popping sound as he shoves me down onto a metal chair. He throws a notebook and a blunt pencil onto the steel table in front of me.

"They want your story of how the homecoming game became an international incident."

"My hand's broken," I remind him.

"Use your left."

"It will take forever."

He shrugs as if to say that's the amount of time I've been allotted.

Record Group No. 17

Addendum

I don't know how long I've been here, only that I haven't seen the sun in all this time. The lights in my cell go on intermittently, sometimes every few seconds, sometimes every hour. I tell time by the changing of the guard. Assuming they work in ten-hour shifts, they've changed sixteen times. I haven't had a warm meal or a shower. The side of my head has healed into a crusty lump. I can't move the fingers on my right hand. I'm not in a cast. My broken knuckles are in a blood-stained bandage. It took me fifteen guard shifts to write my "story" with my left hand.

Every "day" when a new guard comes in, he or she cable ties my hands and takes me to another room with a table and two chairs. Then Jowls comes in. He never gave me his name, but he has an unforgettable double chin that shakes when he's angry. His chins speak his true feelings. There's a name for that, isn't there? Mr. Ebert tried to teach us. Is it personificakation? I'm so tired I can't remember how to spell it. It's when you make a thing do something that a person would. I don't feel like a person anymore.

A new cell today. Bigger. Brighter. Sanitized. But it still smells like fear and forced confessions. There's a window. On the other side there's a pale-faced girl staring at me with black-rimmed eyes through a curtain of stringy, greasy hair. It takes me a minute to realize it's a mirror, not a window. My reflection smiles at me. I's a terrible thing. A grimace doesn't do it justice. She bares her teeth. It's what I see in her eyes that scares me the most. I look down at the table. I can still feel those awful orbs on me. Is that possible? I risk a glance. I was right! She's still looking at me. I look down. My head hits the table, and

I wake up again. It's been like this. Either I'm in a deep state of oblivion, or pain. Nothing in between. When I look at my reflection, I see her grimace grow. She's laughing at me. She won't stop looking at me. I look away, I look back. Her stare is relentless. "Stop it," I beg. "Please, just stop it."

"I'll stop when you tell me the ██████ truth," Jowls says. I never noticed him come in, or maybe he came in during one of those microsleeps.

He asks me the same question he always does. "Why did you shoot ██████?"

I sigh and hang my head. "I told you already."

Just the act of hanging my head makes me micronap. I wake up because he's pulled my head up by my hair. He lets go, and I feel whiplash.

"We—" I begin. "I thought Mr. Reynolds was going to try to kill Kamal's father. I thought if I could just nick him, he'd… Well, people would try to help him. They'd, you know, surround him. No one else who wanted to hurt him could get a clear shot."

"You shot a man to save him. Do you realize how stupid that sounds?"

I do realize that now.

He laughs. "I hope no one ever tries to save my life by putting a bullet through my chest!"

He slams his fists down on the table. It prevents me from falling into another microsleep. "What's the real reason you shot him?"

"I couldn't think of another way," I say quietly.

"Maybe you've done too much thinking. You've got quite the imagination."

"It's all true," I say weakly.

"From your perspective. Let's start from the top."

I nod at the thick folder on the desk, since my hands are tied. Nodding makes me fall again into microsleep. I forget what I was about to say. He pounds his fist on the folder, and I remember. "It's all in there. I'm finished." Do I mean finished with writing, or just finished?

He picks it up. "In this?" He acts surprised; his chins are telling me it's an act. "Do you know what this is?"

I do. I wrote it. He thinks it's my story/statement/confession. It's a love letter. To Axel.

"It's bullshit." He slams it down on the table so hard I flinch. "Do you want me to tell you what's in here?"

I already know.

"It's a sad story about a sad girl who becomes obsessed with the new kid in school. Secret agent, my ass!"

His ass is too big and obvious to be a secret agent, I think.

"You think that's funny?" I must have smiled. I'm not sure. I'm not sure about anything anymore. Honestly, I think I'm going crazy. Maybe I was crazy from the beginning. It's a thought I can hardly bear. Axel is real, I tell myself. That kiss was real. The blood on my hands is real.

Axel comes to me. He's so close I can feel his breath on my face. When I wake up, it's Jowls that I see.

"What's so special about [illegible]?"

"Nothing. Nothing ever happened there, except—" I start thinking about homecoming. It's a jumble.

"Is that why your parents put you there?"

"They didn't put me there."

"How'd you end up then in [illegible]?"

"I woke up there one day."

"So, aliens dropped you there in their big green spaceship."

He looks up as one of his lackeys brings him a tall drink of water. He begins to pour it down his gullet. It reminds me of something. Mrs. Hawkins. The sound of running water made her happy. It makes me desperate. His double chin seems to expand like the twin humps of a camel.

I'd kill for just a sip of it. The only thing keeping me from wrapping my hands around his double chin is the cable tie around my wrists. I lick my lips, it's like running sandpaper over them. My tongue is dry and useless. Or is it? "It was silver," I say in a dry, scratchy voice.

Jowls puts the glass of water down just out of my reach. He writes down the word *silver* on the pad in front of him. "What was silver?" he asks eagerly.

"The spaceship. It wasn't green. It was silver. The aliens had big eyes, skinny necks, and antennae. They had portable translating devices like Google Translate. They wore them as necklaces." If I tell him what he wants to hear, maybe I could have just a drop of that clear liquid.

He bangs his hands on the table, his chins snapping in anger.

"I want the truth not some made-up [illegible]. Do you think I'm stupid?"

"Yes," I say quickly. I'm not going to lie anymore. He bangs the table again. The truth hasn't satisfied him any more than a lie.

"Where are your parents?"

"They're dead."

"That's what they want us to believe."

My heart thuds with hope. It feels like a defibrillator. Could they be alive? It's not possible.

"They're dead or they would have come for me," I say.

"They didn't come back, because they don't love you enough."

I sob. I'm a husk, and no water comes out of my eyes. I make a whispery sound like dry stalks in the wind.

"Or at least that's what I thought at first," Jowls says in a thoughtful tone. "Now that I've gotten to know you, I realize they didn't even like you very much. Did you ever think about that?"

My breath is a desert wind whistling in my lungs. I had thought about it, in my darkest hours, eating lunch in the supply closet, tossing and turning, sleepless in the house of my fake uncle. If my parents had truly loved me, they would have saved me. They wouldn't have let something as trivial as death stop them.

I hate you, I say to Jowls, but what I hear over and over is me saying: "I hate them." It's not my proudest moment. And I know it's probably being recorded and filmed for posterity.

"Maybe they weren't ever planning to come to [redacted]. Where were you supposed to meet, if you got separated? I'm sure your father had protocols."

I say nothing. I want to think it's because I would never give my parents up. It's because I have nothing to give.

"When and where were you supposed to meet? Think! They must have said something!"

I close my eyes. Maybe he'll think I'm concentrating, and he'll let me sleep. But I think about my parents. I can no longer see their faces in my mind's eye, like they've gone undercover from my memory.

"What did they say?" Jowls screams in my ear.

The faces of my parents coalesce for a moment, and I can see them clearly. *Go ahead, tell them what we told you,* they say.

"When and where?" Jowls demands.

I open my eyes. I start speaking fast. He scrambles to get it all down on paper. "Where the pavement ends. Where the crawdads sing."

"What does that mean? In the south somewhere?"

"The blue bayou."

"When?"

"When Jupiter aligns with Mars. In Paradise City."

"I want specifics."

"There is a house in New Orleans."

"You have a street name? A house number?"

"Eight-six-seven-five-three-zero-nine."

"Are those coordinates?"

"That's all I remember."

He gets up. His jowls move like two hands being rubbed together in anticipation. He takes the notebook, and pencil, and the glass of water, and he leaves the room. I put my head down. In an instant I'm asleep.

Jowls is back. I don't know how long he was gone. It could have been a minute or an hour. I'm not refreshed when he yanks my head up off the desk.

"You really think I'm stupid, don't you?" I can't nod the way he's gripping my hair. He lets me go.

"Those are song lyrics and book quotes you gave me."

I hadn't been lying. They were all things my parents had read to me or sung to each other accompanied by the radio in whatever stolen car they were driving at the moment, while I enjoyed the changing scenery in the back seat.

He lets go of my hair. My forehead ricochets off the tabletop, knocking the happy image of my parents out of my mind.

"Do you know what you are?" Jowls loves questions like this. I know what they're called but I can't remember how to spell rutorical. "You're a pathetic loner with no friends and no family, spinning fantasies to make up for the fact that no one loves you."

My parents were real. Axel is real.

Does Jowls read my mind? "This Axel doesn't give a damn about you." He hangs his head for a moment and makes a *tsk, tsk* sound. "Oh, I'm sorry, I made a mistake. I spoke about him in the present tense."

"Axel," I whisper. Dead? Something snaps in me so hard I can hear it. Axel is dead. I start to cry. I've gone without drinking for so long, it takes a couple of ugly choking sobs until liquid comes out of my eyes. My lips are so chapped it stings when my tears touch them. I'm so thirsty, I flick my tongue out to catch them. I hate myself for it. I risk a look at my reflection. She hates me even more.

Jowls watches me for a while. "Now, what do you have to say?"

I don't say anything at all. I'm sobbing, I know my mouth is open, but no noise comes out. "You're right," I say, when I can finally speak again, my breath coming in jags. "I made it all up.

All of it." I cry even harder. I'm not ashamed. I have to get it out. "I'll tell you everything, I'll write out my confession, if you just bring me some paper."

He doesn't smile, but I can tell he feels triumphant. His chins jiggle like they're slapping each other. He goes to the door, opens it, and asks for writing utensils. Part of me wonders how wise it is to have an interrogation room that opens from the inside, but the rest of me is too worn out to care. I lay my head on the cold surface of the desk.

Axel comes in and squats down next to me. He runs his hand over my hair. "I'm here, Talya. I'll take care of you." He disappears as Jowls slams a legal pad onto the desk and a pencil and I wake with a start. I'm so tired. But I have to finish this. Maybe then they'll leave me alone. I can't hold the pencil because my hands are still cable tied. Jowls sighs, goes to the door again, and calls for someone. A suit comes in.

He's not armed, at least not with a gun. Once he cuts me free, I wrestle the box cutter from him and fight my way outside. But it's just a dream again. I no longer have enough liquid in me left to cry. I'm thirsty, I'm hungry, I'm lonely. I'm scary. Scared. I mean scared. I glance at my reflection. I mean both. She's tried to wipe the tears away. All she did was make smudges of the dried blood on her face. She's a savage. With empty, terrible eyes.

"Go ahead, pick it up, or is your hand broken?" Jowls says. It's a cruel joke. I don't laugh; his chins are beside themselves. I pick up the pencil with my left hand. It takes me two tries. I remember saying something to Axel to convince him to train me. That the only weapons I had were my head and a sharp pencil. This pencil is so blunt, I won't have enough lead to write what I need to. I'll have to choose my words carefully. I close my eyes trying to think. I wake again because Jowls is in my face.

"Writer's block? You're usually so damned creative." He's yelling now. I want to tell him, he doesn't have to yell, I'm right here.

Begin at the beginning. It sounds simple, but it's not easy. Who said that? Mr. Ebert. Did he blow up the school? I try to recall one of his motivational posters. In my mind, I look around his room. Every one of them is blank.

I tilt my head back and stare at the tiles in the ceiling. "What are you looking for? Inspiration?" Jowls is so close I could kiss him. The image makes me sick, but I have nothing in my stomach to lose. I have nothing at all to lose.

I count down from ten to a big fat zero. I take a deep breath, bring my head down and hit Jowls on the nose. Hard. His hands go to his face. I stand, knocking my chair backward and I jam the pencil hard into his shoulder. I was aiming for his heart, but he turned. It only goes in part of the way. Either it's not sharp enough, or I hit bone. Either way, he yowls. I don't wait to ask him. The door is unlocked. I'm out in the hallway. I take in box-cutter guy to my right who had been watching through the two-way mirror. I go left.

What do I think my chances are of escaping? Between one percent and nothing left to lose. I have one skill left: being underestimated. I thought I was dealing with professionals. I manage to make it down the hallway and around the corner before being tackled by another uniform. Box cutter jumps on top. I scratch and claw until I can't anymore. If my sparring with Axel was a dance, this is a mosh pit. Now I'm cheek to cheek with the concrete floor. It feels like someone is sitting on me. Maybe someone is. I can't breathe. Things start to go fuzzy, but it's not getting dark. I see light. Is this what people talk about, what they see when they… The light is warm. I haven't seen it in so long I almost don't recognize it. I'm not dying yet. It's sunlight.

I hear a voice that sounds like heaven. "That's enough. Damn it! Let her go."

I can't say a word, my larynx is flat. My heart is expanding. The weight lifts off me and I raise myself to a hunched sitting position. I press my good hand to my stomach. "Axel?" All I can do is repeat his name. He pulls me up. I press my face into his shoulder. He groans. I remember it's his bad shoulder. I don't care.

"You all right?" he asks, reaching toward my stomach. I gasp and bend protectively over it.

The two guards are between me and the door. "Get an ambulance here," Axel says.

Box-cutter man starts to protest.

"Now!"

Out of the corner of my eye I see the man's partner patting his pants for his phone and pulling it out, then feeling around again and cursing. He bends over, scanning the ground as if he's lost something.

"I'm sorry they did this to you," Axel is saying to me. "When I got out of the hospital, they wouldn't tell me where you were."

I pull away far enough to really look at him. The first thing I notice is he's wearing a dress shirt. There's a swatch of blood and snot on it from where my face was pressed against him. His hair is short. His face clean shaven. I had recognized the voice, but this isn't my Axel.

"Are you real?" I ask.

He gives me a crooked smile and the eyes seem more familiar. He doesn't answer the question.

I hear Jowls. His voice makes me shake. "What is this? A hug fest? Subdue the suspect!"

I step away from Axel. It may be the hardest thing I've ever done. I can't stop looking at him, but in the corner of my eye there's Jowls, coming at me. I swing my arm up so it's parallel with the hallway.

He stops dead. I hear sharp intakes of breath around me. Am I that powerful? I can stop him by holding out my hand.

"Talya," Axel says slowly. "Where'd you get the gun?"

"On the floor. I think he lost it." I point with my trigger finger to the uniform who is still patting his pockets. He freezes as the gun moves in his direction. "Always have a plan. You said that. I think you said that."

He holds out his hand. I want to take it, but my good hand is holding the 9mm with the safety off. My knuckles are broken on my bad hand.

"Give it to me."

"Are you real?" I ask him again.

"You know I am."

Do I? "I can't remember you all the way. I can't remember me."

Jowls starts to curse. He's not a very smart man, I think. But smart enough to torture me. To deprive me of sleep, and light, and freedom. To take away the hope that Axel was alive.

"But I remember him." I point with my gun hand at Jowls. He stops cursing.

Axel takes a step toward me. I back away. My hand is shaking, my arm weaving back and forth. Jowls has such a tiny cruel heart; I don't know if I can hit it. Any vital organ will do.

"I'm real. What we had is real."

"Was it true?" I don't wait for an answer. I've gone through too much. I'm at the breaking point. I spill everything. "I love you. So much. I'm tired. So tired. I can't let them do this. I just want to sleep. But he'll never let me." Jowls starts talking again. "Tell him to shut up. Tell him to stop being so [illegible] stupid." I think I'm screaming. I'm not sure. The light is doing funny things, stretching and reforming.

Axel is looking at me. "Don't!" He holds up a hand toward Jowls. "Don't underestimate her."

Jowls does and takes a step closer to me. And death.

I tighten my grip on the handle of the gun. I'm against the wall. Axel in front of me. Jowls to the left. The two uniforms to my right, with only a box cutter between them. Another uniform arrives. Armed. I see the black hole of the barrel in my peripheral vision. I feel nothing. That's not true. I'm full and empty. Maybe I want to feel nothing. I'm beyond exhaustion.

Axel says something to me. I don't understand it, like the words have been twisted around. I bang my bad hand against the wall. The pain gives me a jolt of adrenaline. I'm starting to fade. I won't let them take me back to that cell. I won't let Jowls control me again. I know as soon as I fire, I'll be fired upon. I know it. I don't see another way. I don't have another plan.

"I'm sorry, Axel. I love you."

He doesn't tell me he loves me back. It hurts, but I'm glad in a way. You can't hold love hostage, beat it out of someone like a confession. You'll never know if they really mean it or they're telling you what you want to hear.

Jowls wants to die. He does. Why doesn't he just shut up? I'm so close to pulling the trigger. I'm not sure I want Axel to stop me.

"He deserves it," Axel says, talking over him. "For what he's done to you. But you don't have to shoot him, because I will."

He pulls his gun, trains it on Jowls, and pulls the trigger.

I watch the big man fall. His head bounces on the concrete as if he's made of rubber. Axel doesn't have to take the gun from my hand. I've dropped it. He pulls me to him in a one-armed embrace.

His back is against the wall, his gun waving. "Get a stretcher here. She needs medical attention."

"What about McGillicuddy?"

"He can wait."

That name. There's something about it, but I can't remember. I can't remember anything. I've forgotten already what Axel looks like. I look up at him. He smiles down at me. It's a grim smile, but there's a light in his eyes. He starts to speak to me. His sentences fall apart before they get to my ears. I lay my head against his good shoulder. His steady heartbeat is something I can understand. It tells me—

Record Group No. 18

Voluntary Statement of Talya X.

I don't remember anything that happened after Axel fired that shot. I fell asleep in his arms. When I woke up, I was in a hospital. There was a real cast around my right hand, not just a blood-soaked bandage. An IV tube was coming out of the back of my left hand. I felt like a marionette. I opened my fist and saw a dirty circle of fabric. They must have cut a piece of Axel's dress shirt away. I must not have let him go. I'm not embarrassed to say I still have it. He saved my life. I wondered if I would ever see him again to thank him.

There was a window next to my bed that looked out on a forest. I spent a lot of time watching the crows fly. I couldn't hear their croaking. At night I saw nothing but my reflection. She smiled at me once in a while. I think she meant it to be reassuring. The black holes of her eyes made me look away.

A social worker came to see me. She had short, spiky hair, a direct gaze, and no healing stones. She pulled up a chair. "How are you feeling, Jessie?"

"Jessie?"

She gave me a grim smile. "They tell me the memory issues are temporary. You had quite a blow to your head." She took my chart from the foot of the bed, pulled over a metal folding chair, and sat down. "Jessie Springfield, 99 Floyd Court, Chicago." She looked up. "Ring any bells?"

I nodded. Axel's favorite songs and bands. "How did I get here?"

"You don't remember anything, do you?"

I lie with a shake of my head. I don't want to remember Jowls.

"We don't exactly know what happened to you. You were dropped off here. We don't know by whom. You were dehydrated, malnourished. Looks like you were treated pretty badly. Also looks like you put up quite the fight. You broke two out of five knuckles in your right hand."

"What about my tr—" I almost said trigger finger. "What about my index finger?"

She checked the chart. "I don't think so. Says here third and fourth. The bones were already starting to heal the wrong way. It's going to be a long haul with physical therapy to get you to a point where you can write a novel, but the doctors are optimistic."

I'd already written my story.

"Looks like they tracked down a cousin who gave authorization for the surgeries. Do you remember a cousin?"

I sat up so quickly, the IV pulled at the back of my hand. "Axel Hemmings?"

She glanced down at the chart, then looked up at me with a wince. "Alex Fleming."

I made a noise that was almost a sob.

"Don't worry, everything seems mixed up right now. It will come."

I tried to wipe my eyes with my good hand, but the IV line was too short.

She gave me that upside-down smile again as she stood up. "If things come back to you, you're going to have a lot to process. They know where to find me." She looked me up and down. I realized she was looking for a place to give me a reassuring pat that wouldn't hurt me. She touched two fingers gently to my cheek. "Good luck, Jessie."

"Wait! Am I crazy?"

She gave me a right-side-up smile. This time I believed it. "In my experience, the crazy ones never think to ask that."

When Axel/Alex came to see me, I was still hooked up to the

heart monitor and to an IV in the back of my hand. At least I no longer looked like the horror story girl.

For a moment when I first saw him, I couldn't speak. The heart monitor did the talking for me, chirping like a canary. Axel smiled that sardonic smile. It was the same one he'd focused on me in Mr. Ebert's class the first day I'd met him. The one that made me hyperventilate. Not much had changed. We both glanced over at the screen as the thin white line that was my heart summited Mount Everest.

"Hey," he said, sitting on the edge of my bed.

There were a million things I wanted to say to him.

"Did I kill him?"

"Kamal's father?" He shook his head and smiled. "Nipped him on the left shoulder. Literally a flesh wound. An incredible shot at that distance."

I fell back against the pillows, as the heart monitor began to scream.

"Are you all right?"

I wasn't sure if I ever would be. I didn't tell him—I never will—but Kamal's father? I had been aiming for his right side. My shot crossed over his most vital organ.

"You look pale. I'll get a nurse."

"No!" I reached the end of my IV leash, but I was able to grab a fistful of his dress shirt to keep him there. He gently opened my hand and held it carefully in his.

"I was worried about you."

"I'm okay," I said, but I wasn't sure. "It's over now. I'm free."

"I don't just mean being locked up. It's not easy to shoot someone."

"I didn't know what else to do."

"If you hadn't, Reynolds would have."

"Why?"

"For love."

I remembered what Reynolds had said. That love was a motivator to get someone to do something they didn't want to.

That he would do anything for love. I'd assumed he was talking in the abstract. I hadn't listened. Axel was right. Reynolds was my favorite teacher. I couldn't see past that until I was staring down the barrel of the gun he was aiming in my direction.

Axel told me what they knew so far. "Reynolds had married a translator working for the US army in a country called . At first it was to help her get her immigration papers, but the marriage turned real, at least for him. She was deported last year, right back into a crisis area. A bureaucratic screw-up."

I remembered Reynold's phone conversation I'd overheard. "Let me talk to her," he'd begged. He probably *had* been talking to his mother-in-law.

Axel went on. "That put her in easy reach of terrorist cells. She became a bargaining chip. Reynolds was the perfect candidate to carry out their demands. He had the skills as a sniper. Because of his disability, he'd be underestimated."

"How did he know what the target was?"

"Your fake uncle told him."

"But how did *he* know?"

"Bad luck or good luck depending on the perspective. Kamal's home country is not very stable. His parents wanted to protect him. They sent him to a place where nothing ever happened, where no one would ever find him. To . But the local newspaper did a story on exchange students, more specifically on the only exchange student ever to come to . They don't even have a digital edition. Kamal's real name isn't Kamal, so no one should have recognized him. No one reads newspapers anyway."

"Except my uncle."

"You've seen Kamal's father."

"In a picture on Kamal's phone," I admitted. And through the sights of my rifle. I shivered.

"Father and son look a lot alike. The father is well-known and has a lot of enemies. Your uncle thought he saw something in Kamal. He did some digging. He set up the hit for a price."

"Because babysitting me didn't exactly bring in a lot."

"We don't know how he contacted the terrorist cell, but that ad you saw for an exterminator was them giving him the go-ahead. He didn't want to do it himself. It was a suicide mission. He looked for candidates among the teachers who would have access to Kamal."

"But Kamal wasn't the target."

"He'd been begging his father to come see him play football at homecoming. He wanted to prove himself. That's all he talked about on phone calls home. Those conversations were being recorded."

"I remember what he said: 'I'll show them. After homecoming they won't be able to ignore me any longer.' He was talking about his parents. But I heard him say something about they'll regret not doing what he was asking. That they were going to lose everything."

"He may have been talking to his brother. The brother is first in line. Rumor has it, he'll abdicate if he gets the crown. It seems Kamal was so disgruntled over the lack of attention, he would have done the same. Poor little rich prince."

"I thought you were profiling him because of where he came from. I was the one doing it. You were right when you said I couldn't see what was in front of me. Especially Reynolds. He was my favorite teacher, the only one who noticed me. I didn't want it to be him."

I groaned. "If I'd only seen what was there and not what I wanted to see, maybe none of this would have happened. If I hadn't given Chatham a concussion, Kamal wouldn't have suited up as quarterback. Maybe his father wouldn't have bothered coming."

"Those what-ifs will torture you. You've had enough of that. If I had only listened to you. You were right about so many things, especially the classified ads."

"That's why my uncle came to school for a parent-teacher

conference. He was putting pressure on Reynolds. Letting him know his wife was a hostage."

I remembered the second phone conversation I overheard. The same words: *Let me talk to her.* They were followed up with a promise to eviscerate the person on the other end, who was holding his wife hostage. "I wonder if Reynolds had second thoughts. The last ad I saw for the exterminator, it said: *Last Call. DEADline approaching. Must act now to receive incentive.* That must have been a message to Reynolds. His wife was the incentive. She was going to be dead, if he didn't act."

"In any case, he agreed to what they wanted. What they wanted was for him to explode a bomb under the stadium, then shoot Kamal's father in the chaos. Or vice versa. I don't think they cared about the order or how it was done."

"It doesn't make sense," I said.

"Love is a big motivator."

"No. I mean, the AV room is like a fortress. A bomb wouldn't have done much damage."

"Reynolds had access to the AV room. He could hide components there."

"He's a trained sniper, yet he shot you at close range and didn't kill you," I reminded him.

"He was firing with his left hand."

"He *is* left-handed. I've seen him write on the board enough to know. He fired at me with a telescopic sight and missed by a mile." By a mile, I meant a couple inches.

"I have no sympathy for him."

"I can understand why he did it. What happened to his wife? Is she dead?"

"Our organization was able to extract her. She's at the facility in ██████████."

"Is that where I was held?"

He nodded, and I shuddered. "Why?"

"Leverage. Let's just say Reynolds had information and he proved resistant to certain interrogation protocols."

"You mean the people you work for tortured him, and he didn't give you anything, so they dangled his wife like bait. That technique sounds familiar, doesn't it?" Why was it only considered evil when the other side did it?

"If it weren't for you… You saved my life," Axel said.

"You saved mine."

He shook his head. "They would have let you go eventually."

"That's not what I mean. My world closed in after my parents died. I was living in solitary confinement in my head. You opened the door."

He gave my hand a gentle squeeze.

"Aren't you in big trouble for shooting Jowls?" I asked.

"Jowls?"

"The double chins. The guy who kept me locked up. You said his name, but I can't remember it anymore."

He didn't give me the name now as he explained. "There's been something of a regime change at ████████. A. has taken over. She's tough as nails, but fair. She agreed with me there wasn't much else I could do to diffuse the situation. I shot him to save his life. Using the same technique you used on Kamal's father, ironically."

"So, Jowls didn't die?" I'm not sure how I felt about that.

"Just a flesh wound."

Jowls had so much flesh, that wasn't saying much.

"Why didn't he believe me?" I asked.

"I'm sure he did believe you."

"Then why didn't he let me go?"

"I don't know."

"Who was my uncle?"

"I don't know."

"Or they won't tell you," I guessed.

"You think you still want to pursue a career in this field?"

"You're still asking me?"

He blew out a breath. "If I can't convince you otherwise, let me give you a piece of advice: don't trust anyone."

"Not even you?"

"Especially me." His eyes dropped to my mouth, his expression wistful. He smiled as the heart monitor betrayed me with a beep. *I* won't betray what happened next. Not even under torture.

Axel came to see me again before I left the hospital. I'd been disconnected from the IV and the heart monitor. I was no longer a marionette. It was scary to be free. I knew I couldn't go back to ██████. I didn't know what awaited me going forward.

I was still lying on the hospital bed, but I was dressed in street clothes: sweats, tank, and zip-up hoodie.

When Axel walked in, I was glad I was no longer attached to the monitor. I tried to focus. I still had so many questions. Ebert would have called this the denouement, the scene in which everything is explained.

He was no longer teaching English in ██████. Axel told me his story.

"Ebert had been using the space under the backstage trap door for no good, but it had nothing to do with international terrorism. He was setting up a meth lab even though he understood nothing of the science behind it."

"That explains the missing digital scales, and all those conversations with Ms. Singleton."

"He'd been asking questions about chemistry. Something sparked between them. She encouraged him to give up the whole venture and write a screenplay about it instead. I guess no one told him it had been done before."

I pictured the two of them having kids, boys and girls, all with loose ponytails. "I knew he wasn't the one you were looking for," I said. "Remember what he wrote? *Those kids are going to think different about me.* He's an English teacher. He would have said: *think differently.* So, he was writing dialogue for a play! He wasn't planning on blowing up the school."

"Maybe not on purpose," Axel said. "Meth labs are extremely flammable."

"You never told me what happened to Chatham." I'd been afraid to ask. "I couldn't have done it without him."

"You would have found a way."

I shook my head. "Did they lock him up too?"

"He escaped a life sentence in every sense. He broke up with Darcy."

"Thank god, he's free," I said. Chatham ran through my mind's eye. As he did so, he tore off his tie. And he really did look ~~a little~~ a lot like Superman.

Axel narrowed his eyes as if he could see the images spooling out in my head. "Your *friend* is the hometown hero. Reynolds shot Kamal's father. Chatham shot Reynolds."

"That's not the way it happened."

"It's the official version. Unofficially? I saw the original footage before it was…edited. You were amazing. Absolutely incredible."

Wow, right? Axel thought I was *amazing*! I may have lost a lot in solitary confinement. I'd held onto sarcasm. I registered the compliment, but what rang in my ears—like a fire siren—was how easily the ██████████ could bend reality. How easy it would be to erase me. They *had* erased me. Just like that.

I wondered how long it would take for Axel to forget about me. He stood up. The way he looked at me made me nervous. Intense, like he was trying to memorize my features. I wouldn't have many more chances to talk to him.

"What's going to happen now?" I asked.

"You'll be taken to a secure facility until you're up to full strength. By then, you'll be old enough to decide for yourself what happens."

"Secure? Are the locks on the inside or the outside?"

He didn't answer me. He leaned over and kissed me gently on the cheek. I was glad I was no longer hooked up to any monitors, but I was tired of secrets.

I've tried to avoid clichés. It had been good advice from a teacher I'd trusted, who had turned out to be a potential meth manufacturer. I had to decide for myself what was right. Sometimes what we think is a tired overused phrase is not a cliché, because every time you use it, it becomes new, creates something out of nothing. A connection where there was none.

"I love you," I said to Axel. "From the moment you smiled at me. When you knocked Tommy's head against his desk in English class. When you winked at me…I can't help it."

He reached out and rubbed a finger against my cheek. "You make it sound like it's a bad thing." He leaned in to close the distance between us. "I—"

The door opened with a *thwack*, and he never finished his sentence. Mr. Ebert would call that a cliffhanger. What I wanted to do most at that moment was throw Tommy off a cliff. He stood there in the doorway, half his face covered in gauze.

I had wondered if I would have killed him if someone hadn't pulled me from him under the stadium that day. I no longer wondered.

"Dude, you're a tough girl to find," he said, sounding more nasal than before. "Where were you? CIA sleep-away camp? Solitary confinement? I guess that's the same thing, huh?"

"How did you find me?"

"Been scouring the hospitals for a girl with broken knuckles. You had to show up eventually."

"What the ██████ are you doing here?" Axel asked.

"I'm on desk duty till this heals." He pointed toward his face. "She's like a ██████ plastic surgeon." He didn't seem angry. He seemed much more mellow than usual. I think he was on a bunch of painkillers, and I'm pretty sure he liked it. Some people are way too into their jobs, and when your job involves a lot of drugs…

"I'm here recruiting." He held his hands up like he was measuring distance. His hands didn't quite match up. "I was this close to busting the biggest drug ring on the ██████

coast when all that stuff went down, but, hey, it worked out anyway. Turns out one of those kids that got stepped on had a kilo of [redacted] on him. They found it when they got him to the hospital. He spilled everything."

He pointed at me, or at least in my general vicinity. "Do you know, Axel, or whatever your real name is, she brought you back from the dead? Without paddles. With her [redacted] bare hands. She really is a machine, an honest to God machine."

He focused on me. Or at least he turned his gauzy face to me. I couldn't say his eyes could really focus. "So, Talya, what do you say? Do you want a job?"

What I said really shouldn't be repeated. I couldn't do what I really wanted to because Axel was holding me back. Where would I have rather been? Bashing Tommy's brains in, or in Axel's arms? For a minute, it was a tough choice.

I'd spent a lot of time with Axel but had had so few romantic moments with him. Tommy had ruined a bunch of them. None of the curses I hurled at Tommy were a clear no. He must have understood I had no interest in ever working with him, because at some point he left. I was alone again with Axel.

Would Axel have said *I love you* back? Now was not the time to ask, heh? What were ya gonna say? I relaxed into his embrace. I tried to hear in the beating of his heart what he hadn't said out loud. He held me so tightly it was hard to breathe. His arms told me he didn't want to let me go. His cheek against my hair told me he wanted to be closer. He put his lips to my ear. I don't want to cheapen the moment by repeating what he said to me. It's private. Let's just say, you don't say those kinds of things to a person unless you really care about them. Unless you love them.

He stood, prying my hands gently from his shirtfront. My right was still in a cast. I held on with the tips of my fingers. It hurt to hold him. It hurt worse not to. He gave me a gentle kiss. On the forehead.

With my good hand, I grabbed him by the collar, brought

him back, and we kissed the right way. It was a kiss that lasted. It was sensual and bittersweet, full of longing and unfillable promises.

He pulled away from me. Then he bent his head and kissed me again. Hard. It was a kiss of unsaid things and untold dreams. That, too, had to end. He rested his forehead against mine. We stayed that way for a few moments, him breathing hard, me not breathing at all.

"Remind me not to underestimate you." He touched my cheek. "See you when you're eighteen."

On that promise, I let him go.

Record Group No. 19

Voluntary Statement of Talya X.

I went from the hospital straight to the training facility at ████████. I was given standard-issue clothing: gray sweats, tank top, and a zip-up hoodie. Exactly what I always wore, except now it was a uniform. I felt almost at home.

I met with A. the day I got there. Her desk held nothing but a pen and pencil and a notebook, lined up carefully. There were no knickknacks or family photos. Some might call her office austere. I found it comforting.

The pleasantries didn't last long. She looked at the cast on my right hand and didn't offer her own hand to shake.

"You can start your training today, if that's what you want," she said.

I nodded.

"It will be mostly conditioning, running, a lot of classroom work. No hand-to-hand until you turn eighteen. For practical reasons." She looked at my cast again. The side of her mouth twitched as if in irritation. "And for liability reasons. You're technically still a minor."

She studied me. "I think you should know, we're taking you on despite the recommendation of our field agent ████████, or as you knew him 'Axel.'"

My heart stumbled. Axel had not recommended me? He'd told me he wouldn't, but that was before homecoming. I'd assumed he'd changed his mind.

"Why?" One word was all I could manage.

"The original footage from the incident in ████████ convinced us of your potential. Potential isn't the right word. It showed us what you are capable of. What you've already accomplished. Frankly, we were impressed. We don't often see that kind of power and awareness coming from someone so young."

"I meant why did *your agent* not recommend me?"

She gave away a small smile. "The same reason. Your age. He thinks you're too young. Too vulnerable." She shrugged. She opened a drawer, pulled out a college-ruled red notebook and a stack of bound papers that had dark spots on the covers and placed them on the desk. "I've read your…reports."

I knew those were bloodstains on the covers of my dossier and the statement I'd written in solitary, not heart stickers or unicorns, but I couldn't help being embarrassed. I felt lightyears older than the girl who had written all that.

"*Vulnerable* is not the word I would use to describe you in action. But he felt you had some unresolved issues from your past. He didn't think this was a good or healthy career choice for you." She pushed the papers toward me. "You can have these back now."

"He doesn't know what's good for me. He doesn't know me."

Was it a betrayal? I'm still not sure. Did it break my heart? His dying for a few moments had done that. This in comparison was a bad sprain. They say sprains take longer to heal than a break.

She was watching me with a penetrating look. "You don't think you're joining us for the wrong reasons?"

"Are there any wrong reasons?"

She gave away a bigger smile. "He also warned us not to underestimate you. I wonder if he's guilty of not taking his own advice."

She was watching me closely. "Do you have any questions?"

A million. "Did I kill my uncle? Was he really my uncle?"

"I meant about your training." She sighed. "We don't know the answer to either question definitively. The house has been completely sanitized."

"Was he working for you?"

"Of course not. Based on our agent's description we think his name is—or was—Ivan Ivanov."

"Isn't that just the Russian version of John Smith?"

She shrugged. I'm sure she'd thought of that too.

"He said he was part of my extended family. Do you think that's true?"

"Not on your father's side. We don't know enough about your mother's side to say for sure."

"Do you think he had orders to kill me?"

"We think he had some kind of orders to keep you until you were of age."

I noticed she didn't say *keep you safe.*

"We know he orchestrated Mr. Reynolds' involvement in the potential plot. We think he realized once all hell broke loose, ████████ would be crawling with agents looking for answers. It was no longer safe or comfortable for him to stay there."

"I was a loose end to be tied up before he left." I sat up straight, blazing with awareness. "You know enough about my father's side of the family to know my fake uncle wasn't related. How do you know that? Axel said my parents didn't exist."

"At first, we found no record of them. They were buried deep in the system. We've since been able to uncover some information, now that we know where to look." She steepled her hands in front of her like she was settling in to tell a long sad story. "Maybe it's best I start at the beginning. Our work runs on intuition like any other. Axel is young, but he's got all the right instincts. We took him from high school too. In his first report on his first day in ████████, he mentioned you. He knew there was something…"

She paused.

Please God don't say *special,* I thought.

"…different about you. He did an internet search, and it brought up nothing. Absolutely nothing. That raises red flags.

Everyone has an internet presence no matter how small. He went through the school records. Talya X. had only existed on paper for 1,059 days at that point." She tapped her desk. "His instincts told him something was wrong. He went against protocol by letting you get close, by telling you things."

"He didn't tell me anything," I said.

She tapped the desk twice meaningfully, her fingers saying, *No, that wasn't true.* "Not in so many words. He never should have been teaching you hand-to-hand combat, let alone training you in small arms fire and ballistics." She continued to tap the desk. "He's received a reprimand in his file."

"That's not fair."

She held up a hand. "Let me finish. He's also received a commendation for what he did. Without you acting upon the training he gave you, we would have lost Kamal's father. He's our most important ally in ████████. The only mistake Axel made was putting your picture into the database. But he didn't know what it was going to set in motion. None of us did."

"Why was it a mistake?"

"McGillicuddy was looking for you."

"That name! I heard my father talk about him. I thought he made it up."

"Unfortunately, he's real."

"Why was he looking for me? Axel said I didn't exist."

"You look very much like your mother. McGillicuddy had bots programmed into the database to alert him to any mention of your parents. Facial recognition flagged your picture. He thought you could lead him to your parents."

"McGillicuddy kept asking me where they were. I thought he was trying to break me to get me to change my story about homecoming. He wouldn't accept it when I told him they were dead." I leaned toward her, hope pulling me forward. "Axel said there was no record of any carjacking. Maybe they're not…"

"I'm sorry, Talya." She glanced away just for a millisecond, as if she found grief awkward. "McGillicuddy's beliefs defy logic…and death."

"I don't understand."

"He was obsessed. There was bad blood between him and X."

"Who's that?"

"You don't recognize the name?" She let the question hang there. "He was your father."

"I was right?" My breath came in short jags. "He was one of you?"

She nodded, looking down at her desk as if to give me some privacy. If I let out a sob, she didn't comment on it.

"What did McGillicuddy have against my father?" I asked, when I could speak again.

"Your father was tasked with exfiltrating a captured foreign agent in exchange for one of ours. That prisoner escaped on his watch. The exchange was never made. After that, your father dropped off the grid as well. All the heat came down on McGillicuddy. There was a lot of it. It was something of an international incident apparently."

"When was that?"

"About eighteen years ago."

Right before I was born. I opened my mouth to ask a million questions. She cut me off.

"That's all I know." Her voice wasn't exactly harsh, but it was obvious that part of our discussion was closed. Her tone softened as she went on. "It turns out your father was something of a legend around here before that operation. He was one of the best. Don't feel you have to live up to that."

"I don't expect to be treated differently."

"You were, though, weren't you?"

I experienced a short but intense flashback of my six days, five hours, and three minutes with ~~Jowls~~ McGillicuddy. I tried not to let it show.

"You're not going to get an official apology from this organization. But you will from me."

I blinked as she went on.

"I'm sorry."

"It wasn't your fault."

She glanced away again. As if, maybe, she'd done something to feel guilty about. I don't think she was lying to me. Maybe she wasn't telling me everything. I remember Axel telling me not to trust anyone. Not even him. I thought about the things he'd said. I thought about the things that weren't said. I thought about the way he'd kissed me. You can't lie with kisses like that. Or could you?

"It *was* real," A. said, and I wondered if I had spoken aloud. "Axel cared." She corrected herself. "He cares."

"You don't know that."

"I've read all of his reports. And yours. I've been in this business long enough to be able to read between the lines. He risked his career, maybe even his life, shooting McGillicuddy who was technically his superior. You don't do that, unless you care about someone."

I didn't know what to think. So, I stopped thinking at all. I stared at those pages on her desk, which I had written. All the facts were there. Would they ever add up?

"This is a lot to process," she said into the silence. "I'm sorry. Deeply and truly sorry that this happened to you, that you suffered at our hands. I can't offer anything more than that…with the exception of extensive counseling during your training."

"I don't want counseling." I said it with so much emotion, that even I had to admit, I could probably use it. A lot of it.

"It's part of the deal. Our agents need to protect themselves from any outward threat, but there's a danger from within as well. The things you've experienced can tear a hole in you from the inside." She stared me down. I stared back. "They can turn a logical person into a ticking time bomb."

Axel had said she was tough as nails. Her eyes were steely. "It's mandatory." I heard some steel in her voice as well. Again, it took on a softer tone. "The healing stones are optional." She didn't smile, but I swear the light glinted off the nail heads that were her pupils. Nails can go straight through you. She'd put a couple right into my heart. She would have called it being honest. As she held my gaze, I think she was trying to show me how nails could hold things in place, keep them from falling down.

I considered my options. Since I didn't have any, it didn't take long for me to blink. I had missed deadlines for applying for college. I wasn't getting a dime in scholarships or financial aid. Now I know why my uncle didn't want to reveal his tax returns. Because they didn't exist. He didn't exist. I could get a job, but I had nowhere to live. I had nowhere else to go.

A. knew that, just like she knew (almost) everything else about me. Without a word, she stood and offered me her left hand to shake. I took it. It wasn't as awkward as you'd think. I felt she was trying to offer me something more than just a job with that firm but warm handshake. Welcoming? Belonging? Not being so familiar with either, they were hard to recognize. These were not normal feelings for me. Maybe, with enough time and distance (and counseling) under my belt, just maybe, they could be good ones.

Epilogue and New Beginnings

I have a room of my own at the [redacted] training facility. My window looks out on a concrete courtyard. It's like a prison cell, but I don't feel trapped. I feel like I'm on the edge of something vast. I think it's called possibility. Today was a long day, not the longest or hardest I've ever had. We started hand-to-hand combat training. I feel physically tired, but something in me is wide awake. It's late. I don't want to go to sleep. I stand at my window. It's gotten cold, but the year will end without having touched any snow.

I don't wear glasses anymore, except for target practice, for safety reasons. I no longer feel the need to hide behind them. I'm being trained in all manner of arms, anything that can expel a projectile from bows to bayonets. When it came to using silencers, I got emotional. Not because it reminded me of the carjacking; because it didn't. It wasn't the sound I remembered. My recollections of that time are fading. The faces of my parents are fading.

I still see their bodies turning to ragdolls. I see Kamal's father tumbling backward in the bleachers. Not all the flashbacks are bad. Right now, there's still a spot of brilliant blue in the sky. I see Chatham's clear compassionate eyes. I think of the poem he wrote. I see now it was for me. I still have the scrap of it in my dossier. I never gave him back that piece of his heart. Does he know he has a piece of mine?

I think about Mr. Reynolds a lot, who believed all the right things and did all the wrong ones. For good reason? For love? I knew what it was like to be willing to do anything for someone you care about. I was just glad I didn't have to decide between a school full of kids and a lover. I try not to think about what I'd be willing to do for my parents.

Slowly, the evening draws pink swatches across the sky like it's putting on makeup, getting ready to go out. I still don't wear makeup. Although this is a big night, I'm not going anywhere. I stay at my window keeping watch, seeing the old year out. A year that changed me.

The day goes to bed. I can't. It's dark outside and all I can see is my own reflection in the window. She flexes her left hand, which is actually my right hand. She's turning it into a fist over and over. I can tell by the way she winces that it's sore.

Muscle memory is a funny thing, although I don't think the instructor today found it all that funny. When he came at me, memory of my training with Axel kicked in. I kicked him into the wall. I didn't stop there. A classmate tried to step between us. Let's just say what happened next hurt me more than it did him. His jaw is the first thing I've hit since breaking my knuckles. The pain doubled me over. I won't see the instructor tomorrow or my classmate because of their concussions. Also, I need more physical therapy. After that I'm being moved into the advanced class.

By the way, I didn't apologize. Axel taught me well.

Axel. I haven't seen him since the hospital. My reflection doesn't seem surprised. The corner of her mouth makes a furtive movement, but her expression remains calm. I'm sure I could track him down. *Hunt him down*, my reflection seems to say. She had been so gullible and had felt so hurt, I'm afraid she'd want to eviscerate him. That's not a euphemism. It means tear his guts out. She thinks our heart is a traitor for the way it still feels about him.

I try not to be so hard on my heart. It's been through a lot. Loving is loss. Or that's been my experience. But it's a loss to not love at all. It's complicated. It's messy. It's free verse, and it's hard to understand. I shrug, and my reflection relaxes her shoulders too. Her hand is still a fist.

I've had a lot of classwork here and homework. I'm not big on the social scene, so I've spent time going over my ~~confession~~,

~~interrogation~~, ~~interview~~ story. I've been reading between the lines. I misread Chatham. Because he was "normal," I couldn't see how awesome he was. And how true. I wonder if I'll ever see him again. I never said goodbye. I never said thank you. There's so much more I never said. I wonder if he thinks of me. I hope he knows that I think of him. I can never go back to the town of ██████████, but, maybe, someday he'll get out of there, and I'll see him again.

And Axel?

I've been reading him in a different light, in which he knew everything about me, more than I knew about myself. Some passages I read make me feel like he's with me again. I feel his eyes on me, I feel the warmth of his lips. I feel the truth in all that. But the truth is he's never once contacted me since I've been here. I thought today might be the day. I finished re-reading my story last night. I remember now he said: "See you when you're eighteen." He did not say *as soon as you turn eighteen.*

I should be grateful to him. I won't say he made me what I am; he helped me get to who I am. He made me stronger, more aware. He taught me to shoot straight. Someday he may regret that.

He taught me how to open my heart again. Taught me how much that hurts.

I see now how he tried to protect me, by pushing me away. It's as crazy as shooting a man to save his life. He was also trying to protect me from himself. I think the footage from ██████████ shows I don't need protecting. But that evidence doesn't exist anymore.

In therapy, I've learned to recognize my emotions. I've learned to name them. It's supposed to take some of their power away.

I loved Axel. I still do. I also hate him.

My reflection is conflicted too, I see it in the furrowed brow. I smooth it away. I can live with conflict. I can live with her. I like her. As more than a friend. We both find that funny.

"Happy birthday, by the way," I say to her. I think how she's grown up. There's something different about her I can't quite put my finger on. "Confidence," she says out loud. I blink at her twice, she blinks back the same amount. She smiles at me. It's a normal smile. Normal isn't such a bad thing anymore. I smile back.

I turn to my bed, pull the covers back and see the envelope lying there on the mattress. Remember what I said about my heart being a traitor? It starts beating against its cage, making all kinds of confessions. Good thing my reflection can't see it. She'd have it taken out and shot. I decide to keep its secrets. I still believe in due process. Mr. Reynolds believed in due process too, I remember. That didn't mean he practiced it.

There's a message scrawled on the front of the envelope.

Couldn't stay. I'm sorry. I've been assigned out of the country. Glad to see you're not pulling your punches (or your kicks). Happy birthday. This is not a present. There are things you should know. Never forget the most important: don't trust anyone. PS I hope you know it wasn't my intent to hold you back. I ~~wanted~~ want so much for you to have a normal life.

I'm only ~~122 days~~ four months older than the girl who used to hang on Axel's every word. In many ways, I'm a different person. In some ways, I'm still that girl. I read through his words again. I notice how he has drawn a line through "wanted," how he has changed the past to the present. I wonder if that means there could be a future? Or if I can forgive him for wanting me to have a normal life.

How could he not have known what normal meant to me? I realize how few things I had said out loud. I hold the envelope to my heart for a minute. You might say I hug it. I'm not ashamed of my emotions. Not anymore.

I open it carefully, so as not to tear the paper. I pull the pages out slowly and gasp as I see the grainy picture on the first page of a stack of photocopies. The name at the top I don't recognize. But I have the same eyes.

I trace my father's strong jaw with my finger. I used to do

that as a kid, except then it was stubbly or thick with a beard. Here he's clean shaven. He's serious, younger. He's got that same something about him I'd always sensed but couldn't name.

Something falls away from me. It's just the shadow of a doubt. Even that had been too heavy to bear. Proof. It took me so long to find it. It's only paper, yet it's solid, something I can hold onto. My father had always been true. True to me, true to my mother, true to his principles. Now I know what he did was also real. Maybe it does have something to do with the letters in bold just before his name that say SPECIAL AGENT. He was exactly what I thought he was.

I'm still staring at my father's picture, but he starts swimming. I wipe my eyes with the back of my hand and go to the next page and the next. At the very back of the stack there's a grainy black-and-white picture from a surveillance camera of a woman whose name I don't know. But those high Slavic cheekbones are the ones she gave to me. I know it's my mother, yet somehow, I still don't recognize her. There's an expression on her face that I've never seen, a look that could kill. Even that doesn't appear as deadly as the gun in her hand. The camera has caught a tendril of smoke curling from the end of the short barrel. I can almost hear the puff and smell the gunpowder as my illusion bursts. This is my mother who didn't believe in guns? There had obviously been a time, before I knew her, when she did believe in them, very strongly.

I have a flashback to what A. told me, about my father botching the return of a foreign agent. I am as guilty of systemic inequality as the next girl. I had assumed the agent was a man. Could it have been my mother? That would mean they were enemies, my parents.

But they loved each other. Fiercely. You can't fake that for fourteen years. Can you?

I would give anything to know what happened back then. The problem is I don't have anything to give. They left me with nothing. That's not true, though, is it? They gave me love, and I still have it, or at least the memory of it. I start to read the words now that accompany the photos. I've never had this much information. Information means possibilities. Knowledge is power. Power is not something I am used to having.

I go to the window, putting the papers back into the envelope. There is one I overlooked. It's a medical report. Mine. I don't understand the jargon, just the gist. I have an entrance wound and an exit wound, but no internal scarring. That means I wasn't shot. I was made to think I'd been shot.

I think of the silencers I'm being trained to use now. I think about how they sound different than the silencers used in the carjacking. I think of the training I've had in non-lethal tactics. I've learned how dart guns work. How they use compressed gas to fire a ballistic syringe. How a steel ball in the syringe, activated by momentum, pushes the plunger down and injects on impact. I've never heard it fired. At least not in training. But three years ago, during the carjacking?

I was tranquilized, not shot through with a bullet. I feel betrayed. Fooled. I realize what that could mean. That my parents were tranquilized too. That they're alive!

I try to tamp down my excitement, but it vibrates through me, making my hands tremble. I'm afraid to believe it. I remember A.'s reaction. When I said my parents were dead, she didn't confirm it; she looked away. I thought grief made her awkward. Maybe she knows something she won't or can't tell me. Axel told me not to trust anyone.

I have too many questions and not enough answers.

If my parents did survive—if—I don't know where they were taken or what was done to them. They could have been tortured. They could have been killed later. I'm afraid to hope.

Hope doesn't care how I feel. It takes root. Along with something just as powerful. It's still dark outside. I can see my reflection clearly. I can tell she's been crying. What I notice most is the hard line of her mouth, the set of her jaw.

I've come to know ~~her~~ myself much better in the last

months. Extensive therapy has helped me to look back at the charred landscape of my last three years. The words "scorched earth" come to mind.

There's something rising now from those ashes. I've heard its song before like the cawing of the crows, but never this strongly. There is nothing garden-variety about a Phoenix.

I'd assumed it was the love I had for my parents that kept me alive, even after they couldn't love me back. There had been something else there, beneath all that, next to it, hopelessly entwined with it. It forced me to get up in the mornings. It propelled my feet forward one after the other. It kept the electrical pulse beating in my heart.

My heart feels like it will explode.

There's an energy crackling through me, screaming along my nerve endings. I know now what has driven me, kept me alive. Naming it does nothing to take away its patient power. I feel its seduction. An overwhelming hunger. The white-hot desire. For revenge.

It is burning away the old me. It's making me new. Birth is an awesome and terrible process that we can't remember. Rebirth is no different, except there is no forgetting. It is agonizing. Energizing. Violent. Victorious. I know what I am capable of. I know what I want. I know who I am. My name means birth, after all.

I swear I will find my parents. I will find the people who separated us. And I will make them regret it.

Outside my window, the dawn of a new year is electrifying the edge of the horizon. The sun, when it shoots a ray over the edge of the darkness, ignites a spark in my eye before my reflection fades against the coming light.

My heart throbs as if it is learning to beat for the first time. It is not an easy lesson. I put my hand over it, feel it settle finally into a powerful but controlled rhythm. Like the ticking of a time bomb.

Acknowledgments

Bibi Wein has guided so much of my writing, including this manuscript. Suzanne Stewart read the first draft. Nev March's webinar on "How to Write Layered Stories" was the blueprint for a major revision. Thank you to Skip Fischer for reviewing my contracts. Adirondack Center for Writing has been a constant source of information and opportunities, as is the Author's Guild and Marcela Landres' Latinidad.

This book was informed by my own high school experience, and years of teaching at the secondary and college levels. I especially thank my students and coworkers. Mr. Kudrich, coach of the Wallenpaupack Area High School rifle team, taught me everything I know about marksmanship and sportsmanship.

I referred to the website TVTropes for quirky spy tricks, the Wildlife Conservation Network for details about dart guns, and Dr. Matthew Green's article in The Londonist "A Grim and Gruesome History of Public Shaming" about torture in the Middle Ages.

Thanks to the city of Freiburg, Germany, where I wrote the first draft, and to the Town of Chester Library and the Coy Library. I appreciate Jaynie Royal and the team at Regal House Publishing and Fitzroy Books for taking on this project. My mom was my first reader and championed every version of the manuscript. Thank you to my husband David—for everything, especially for building a house with two stories where I could write my own stories, and to August and Emma for filling that space with happy memories.